DARK
LAKE

LOUISE
GAYLORD

NATIONAL AWARD-WINNING AUTHOR

Things are rough in the Adirondacks. In fact, they're murder.

DARK
LAKE

An Allie Armington Mystery

LITTLE MOOSE PRESS
BEVERLY HILLS, CALIFORNIA

Little Moose Press˙
269 South Beverly Drive, Suite #1065
Beverly Hills, CA 90212
(866-234-0626)

This is a work of fiction. Names, characters, places, and incidents either are the product of the author's imagination or are used fictitiously, and any resemblance to actual persons, living or dead, business establishments, events or locales is entirely coincidental.

First Edition

Hardcover Edition: 978-0-9841441-9-8
Trade Paperback: 978-0-9838386-0-9
Ebook: 978-0-9838386-1-6
Audio book: 978-0-9838386-2-3

Library of Congress Control Number: 2011912333

Publishers Cataloging-in-Publication Data

Gaylord, Louise.

   Dark Lake : an Allie Armington mystery / Louise Gaylord. -- 1st ed. --
Beverly Hills, Calif. : Little Moose Press, c2011.

      p. ; cm.

      ISBN: 978-0-9841441-9-8
   Summary: After 15 years, Allie Armington returns to her Aunt
Sallie's cottage retreat in the Adirondacks where she spent most of
her childhood summers. But instead of the happy reunion she's
anticipating, she finds murder.

      1. Armington, Allie (Fictitious character)--Fiction. 2. Women
lawyers--Fiction. 3. Adirondack Mountains (N.Y.)--Fiction.
4. Mystery fiction. I. Title.

PS3607.A986 D37 2011   2011912333
813/.6--dc23   1109

Printed in the United States of America on acid-free paper.

Book Design by Dotti Albertine

for the Cohen sisters

My heartbeat quickens as I turn off Route 12 onto Route 28 at Alder Creek and begin the familiar climb toward the Adirondack Park.

It's been fifteen years since I last made the trip. Fifteen years since I was sent packing, head bowed in shame. Now, as my rental car careens around the bends of Route 28, I can't help but feel a twinge of excitement in the pit of my stomach. But there's something else, too. Something I can't quite identify. Something that makes my hands shake a little as I grip the steering wheel.

I brush it off. It's just nerves, I tell myself. Nerves at being back here after so many years. What else could it be?

I force myself to take in the sights flying by outside the window. Despite a crunchy chill in the air, the birch leaves are full blown. White daisies nod their heads at the passing traffic. And occasional clumps of daylilies stand at attention.

I weave through the hamlets of White Lake and Otter Brook and then cross the bridge at the Moose River. After what seems like forever, Thendara and Old Forge, still much the same as I remember, pass quickly and the final part of my journey begins along the north edge of the Fulton Chain of Lakes.

My pulse is now on double time as I slow and turn right to pass between the tall stone columns bearing a small brass plate reading: HOTANAWA.

Meant to sound like a Mohawk Indian name, Hotanawa was cobbled together from the first two letters of four Chicago families' last names: "Hoh" from Holden, "Tah" from Taylor, "Nay" from Napier, and "Wah" Walton.

The road, brightly dappled with late afternoon sunlight for a hundred or so feet, darkens beneath a thick canopy of tall pines and hemlocks as the descent toward Fourth Lake begins.

At the first plateau, I brake for a second, then drive slowly past the familiar landmarks of my teens. After all this time, I still feel that surge of excitement I first felt when our car traveled down the drive so many years ago. And yet this time, it's not as light or innocent as it once was. Now there's a darker edge.

To my right, the fountain comes into view, its faithful artesian well still pulsing water high into the air to arc gracefully and splash into the wide, shallow basin.

Thinking back, I remember the warm days when the gang wasn't dockside, and how the fountain's tumbling waters brought us welcome relief following fierce tennis competitions or a prolonged game of Olly Olly Oxen Free.

The fountain was where I got my first kiss. That kiss had been coming ever since Fin Holden finally "discovered" me on the deck overlooking the moonlit lake. I can still hear the boom box blasting that great 5th Dimension song, "Up, Up and Away," and I can still picture couples, young and old, gyrating to its rhythms.

To my left is the tennis court. It's empty now—not at all unusual this early in the season. And yet, for some reason, its emptiness seems strangely foreboding as I pass it by.

Though some families come up for weekends in June, the compound will not be filled until just before the Fourth of July when everyone arrives to savor the joys of this magical place until the last sad goodbyes are exchanged on the Tuesday after Labor Day.

I make a sharp turn to the right.

Almost there, almost there.

It's my childhood voice chanting as I trembled then with excruciating excitement, and tremble even now. And then another voice, older sounding, whispers words of caution that are lost on the wind.

I gun the motor to urge my rental up the steep hill and the cottage perched above the lake.

Holden Cottage is the only one in the compound that is set apart. The parcel of land along the north shore of Fourth Lake had been purchased by the Holden family in the late eighteen hundreds, and they exercised their right to take first option: the high bank overlooking the lake.

The other three cottages are situated on a flat shelf of land halfway from the highway to the boathouse.

Though the cottages are all within a few yards of one another, well-matured stands of birch and blue spruce offer each of the three families complete privacy.

I pull into the parking space next to a silver 1988 Toyota Land Cruiser. Even after fifteen years, seeing that car triggers a grim reminder the accident.

A shudder begins at the top of my spine as I remember the day Uncle Aiden drove my sister Angela and me to Utica and then west on the New York Thruway to the Syracuse airport where we were deposited curbside in disgrace.

Apparently fifteen years hasn't been long enough. Although Arlene's original invitation had been for the end of June, my cousin called in late March and asked me to push my visit to mid-June, saying she had a big surprise and couldn't wait to tell me about it.

The date change was fine by me. For as long as I could remember Aunt Sallie always opened Holden Cottage the week before Memorial Day, and then spent the month of June enjoying the solitude of her aerie perched above Fourth Lake. For as long as I can remember, Uncle Aiden spent June in Wilmette. Why should this summer be any different?

I shift gears into park and stare at the Land Cruiser for a moment. As I do, an eerie feeling starts somewhere in my gut. I can't shake the nagging feeling that something isn't right. But nothing seems to be amiss. I shrug off the feeling, pop the trunk, and drag out my roller-bag.

I cross the road and struggle down the steep stone steps to the wooden deck. There is a handrail but it still wobbles. That handrail has been at the top of Uncle Aiden's summer project list since forever.

I walk to the kitchen door, a sliding glass door that my dad and his brother installed the first summer we visited. It gave the dark kitchen added light and a pleasant cross-breeze on the rare warm days.

"Hello?"

No answer.

The kitchen, usually filled with the welcoming clang of cooking utensils and ever-enticing aromas, is eerily silent. I choke down my worry, assuring myself that I'm just being silly; that nothing is wrong.

I slide open the screen, step into the darkened room, and stop.

When the small voice at the side of my mind whispers, "Things aren't right," I call out: "Arlene?"

"Aunt Sallie?"

"Anybody?"

I stanch my rising panic, take a long breath, and tell myself that the women are probably at the Big M stocking up on groceries for the weekend. But that can't be. The Toyota is in the parking lot. But then I remind myself that Arlene must have a car.

I make the quick trip through the kitchen to the back hallway, drop my roller-bag on the bottom stair step, and return to open the refrigerator door to see Aunt Sallie's signature pitcher of lemonade crammed with lemon and orange slices sitting on the bottom shelf. I've been dreaming about that pitcher of lemonade ever since I boarded the plane in Houston and that welcoming "gift" suddenly makes everything all right.

I pour a glass, take a swig, and make my way outside to the deck.

It's an unusually warm day for this time of year, and a gentle breeze stirs the budding trees. I flash back to summer afternoons spent with Aunt Sallie long ago, the way she would always ask about, and then praise, my achievements of the past year. She always encouraged me to study harder, play better golf, or pursue any goals I mentioned. I loved her for caring because my mother never bothered to ask me about anything. My mother has never cared enough to bother.

I move to the railing, recalling how often I had leaned against the warm wood to inhale the sweet air rising from the lake. Then my gaze wanders to the narrow sand beach.

Bitter bile lunges to my throat as black spots spire before my eyes and my treasured glass of lemonade drops from my hand to shatter on the moss-covered outcropping below.

Overcome with horror I push away, take a few deep breaths, and then force myself to look a second time.

Thirty feet below, the upper part of her body face down in the frigid waters of Fourth Lake, lies my beloved Aunt Sallie.

CHAPTER 2

I hurry across the deck and through the kitchen to the wall phone in the back hallway. With trembling fingers I manage to pull the heavy rotary dial to 9-1-1.

After identifying myself as a guest of the Armington family at Hotanawa, I give brief details, directions to where I've just seen Aunt Sallie's body, and add that I'm a practicing attorney and a licensed private investigator.

I ask that the police immediately be notified, adding, "There's no need for a siren. The victim is dead. And this doesn't remotely look like an accident. It screams murder."

I hang up, and only then does the reality of the situation hit me. I am too heartbroken to cry, too devastated to scream. I can do nothing but stare blindly ahead, my mind gone blank. I marvel at my ability to string together complete sentences just moments before. Minutes pass as I try to gather my wits about me, failing miserably.

That horrible vision of my beloved Aunt Sallie will be burned in my memory forever. Her long hair, released from the confines of the ubiquitous bun at the nape of her neck, fanned across the surface of the water; her arms, once one of my major sources of comfort, flung wide.

Did she jump? The thought only surfaces for a moment, before I realize how absurd it is. Suicide? No. No. Not Aunt Sallie.

Then and only then do I remember my cousin. "Oh my God," I say out loud, unable to quell the panic in my voice. "Arlene."

Is she in the house, hurt or wounded? Has she been taken somewhere else? And then the worst possibility comes to mind, despite how hard I try to push it back: Will I find her lifeless body, too?

I step woodenly out of the kitchen and into the hallway. The house is eerily quiet. Somewhere in the back of my mind, I realize that the person or people who murdered Aunt Sallie might still be lurking in the house. But I'm not thinking about my own safety. All I'm thinking about is finding Arlene.

I creep slowly into the living room, where I see an overturned chair at the desk. A couple of drawers are half-opened, the contents rifled through.

Why didn't I see this before? Then I remember dumping my bag on the bottom stair step in the back hallway and returning to the kitchen for that much-anticipated glass of lemonade.

A creak over my shoulder makes me whirl around, the hair standing up on the back of my neck. I freeze, unable to move. My heart is pounding. Is someone in the house? Am I being watched? I wait a moment, fearing the worst. But when no one emerges, I tell myself this is just the nature of an old house, full of creaky floorboards and the wind whistling through cracks in the walls.

Stop wasting time, I tell myself impatiently. *You have to find Arlene.*

I walk tentatively up the stairs, expecting the worst with every step. At the top, I move slowly to the bedroom at the end of the hall, the one Arlene and I had shared since my very first visit to Holden Cottage.

The door is closed.

I look over my shoulder again, unable to shake the feeling that I'm not alone. No one is in the hallway. I raise my hand to knock.

The first time I knock there's no response. Then I try again and say, "Arlene, it's Allie. Are you in there? Please answer me."

At the sound of a moan, I turn the knob and slowly swing the door open.

Arlene is in her usual nightwear of a sweatshirt and leggings, but her arms are tied behind her. She lies motionless on one of the twin beds, eyes staring blankly at the ceiling.

Arlene has been on the heavy side since childhood and she was round the last time I saw her at Thanksgiving. Not this Arlene. She's practically skin and bones.

"Arlene," I murmur, trying not to get too choked up.

She looks up at me and the tears come. "Thang Ga, ish you."

Her words are so slurred I can barely understand her.

"Are you all right? You sound like you've been drugged."

"Whe's Mawmah?"

I sit beside my cousin and put my arm around her shoulder. "There's been an accident."

"Nooo. Nooo. Nooo." Her wails fill the room.

I clasp her bony body to mine until her sobs subside enough for her to blurt out, "Mawmah 'n I ha ba figh las nigh. I fell sleep just a sun com up. I her noise. Though you come early. Door open. Wasn' you tall."

"Take it slow, okay?"

Arlene takes an enormous shuddering breath before she gets out her first understandable words. "Two men. Ski masks. Tied arms behind my back. Gave me shot."

When she struggles to her feet, then wobbles uncertainly, I grab for her, pulling her back to the bed. "It looks like you've been drugged and the effects haven't worn off quite yet."

I wait until Arlene has calmed, but when I release my hold, she slithers out of my reach and lunges for the door.

I'm only a few steps behind as she caroms off the wide hall walls, then staggers down the steep narrow stairs. When she pauses in the back hallway, I catch her arm.

"You don't need to see this, Arlene. Why don't you change into something else and we can wait in the kitchen?"

"No! Let me go." She breaks free and heads through the kitchen for the deck.

I catch up, get a solid grasp on my cousin's arm, and pull her to a halt. "Please. Let me go first."

Arlene tries to free herself, but she's in no condition to put up much of a fight.

"Please, Arlene. Don't go to the railing without me, okay? Once we both get there we can face it together."

Arlene searches my eyes, then asks, "It's that bad?"

I nod. "Yes, Arlene. It's that bad. But, I'm here for you. Please let me help you get through this."

She lets out a long breath, then nods, and we cross the deck together.

To my relief Aunt Sallie's body has been pulled from the lake and covered. She's surrounded by several policemen, two EMTs, and a couple of men in civvies. They look up at me and make eye contact. I nod.

Once Arlene realizes what has happened, she tries to drag me toward the stairs leading down to the lake. "I have to be with her. We have to go down."

Again, I dig in my heels until she can no longer resist. Then I point to the yellow crime scene tape surrounding the area where Aunt Sallie lies. "We need to let the police do their job. It won't take long, I promise."

What I don't say is that the police won't let either one of us past that tape until forensics is finished with the site inspection.

I watch as Arlene tries to compute my words, and when she finally does, she nods. "Shouldn't we tell them about the two men?"

When I realize Arlene seems to have regained some sense of rationality, I guide her across the deck toward the picnic table. "Of course we will. But first, let's sit here for a few minutes, okay? I need to make a plan."

Once we've settled, I tick down the crime scene procedure list remembered from my assistant DA days in Houston. The cottage hasn't been declared part of the crime scene, but it will be as soon as the police realize that it's involved. And once the cottage is included, we won't be let back in. I'm sure of that.

I turn to my cousin. "As soon as they're finished down there, the police will put this cottage off limits as well. That means we'll be sleeping someplace else tonight and maybe tomorrow.

"Go to your room. Get some things together and come to the kitchen as quickly as you can. Do not—I repeat, do not—touch anything that might be considered evidence. Got it?"

Arlene gives me a slow nod, then lurches for the kitchen.

After she disappears inside, I slowly rise and drift across the deck to the kitchen, and then to the back stairs where my roller-bag waits.

Once Arlene comes down the stairs, I point her toward the breakfast table, then open the cabinet and pull out the familiar tea tin. "If I remember you like Constant Comment."

"No tea. I need a . . ."

Her voice trails off. I turn her way, tea tin still clutched between my hands. "A what?"

Her eyes widen for a second as she stammers, "A drink. I meant I need a drink."

"Oh, Arlene, do you really think . . ." My voice fades as I read the misery in her eyes.

I head to the living room and the inlaid Victorian commode in the corner.

Uncle Aiden has always prided himself on his large collection of single malts. When the summers ended he would leave the half-empty bottles on the marble top. Sad to say, the marble, a lovely color once, is now stained with dull circles—evidence of summer sloshes followed by the intense winter cold. I remember once asking why he left the partially filled bottles out. And he shrugged. "Alcohol doesn't freeze. No need to stow."

I grab the nearest bottle and head back to the kitchen.

Arlene drains the first shot before I can settle in the chair across from her at the breakfast table. "Is there anybody else in the area that we should notify?"

She looks down, then shrugs.

"What about the other Holdens?"

She looks up to search my face for a second before she murmurs, "I'm surprised you'd even ask about them. No one—" She pauses. "—except for me, has seen much of that family since . . . since the accident."

I'm shocked that, after all this time, I still feel that long ago surge of remorse. "But it *was* an accident, Arlene. You were there."

"Yeah. Whatever." She shrugs and lifts her glass for a refill.

I have just poured her second shot when there's a knock. I look out to see a man in uniform standing at the door to the living room. "Over here, sir. We're in the kitchen."

He crosses the deck and extends his hand. "I'm Chief Zandt, town of Webb Police. Are you Miss Armington?"

"I'm Miss Armington's cousin Alice. She's in here."

Zandt follows me into the kitchen and leans across the table to shake Arlene's limp hand. He offers his condolences, and then turns to me. "And you're here because ...?"

"Not because of this—though I am an attorney as well as a licensed private investigator. I assure you nothing has been touched in the cottage since I discovered Aunt Sallie's body."

He goes into police mode. "Guess we'll find out about that later, won't we? Did your cousin call you? Are you acting as her attorney?"

"No sir. My cousin didn't call me. I arrived just this afternoon from Syracuse, where I spent the night after flying up from Houston."

"You came all the way up here from Texas? That's a joke. June is nothing but black flies and cold fronts."

"Tha's righ', officer. I 'vited her," Arlene slurs, as she attempts to stand. But gravity wins and she slumps back into her chair. From the glazed look on her face it's obvious the Scotch, added to whatever drug is left in her system, has done its job.

An EMT appears in the doorway and begins to check Arlene's vitals. He doesn't get very far before she waves him off. "I'm fine," she says, in a tone that brooks no argument. He looks at the chief, then at

Arlene, then back at the chief before disappearing out the door.

The chief takes the chair next to Arlene and points me to one of the others.

"Again, let me say how sorry I am for your tragic loss, Miss Armington."

When Arlene gives him a mute nod, he continues. "The evidence technicians have just arrived and will be covering the crime scene on the beach, but I just learned from the EMT that you were somehow involved. Is this true?"

"Involve? You th-think I was involve?" Arlene slurred.

Arlene breaks into sobs.

I rush to her side to comfort her and give the chief my most indignant look. "Isn't that a little out of order, sir? My cousin's just learned her mother is dead and you accuse her of complicity?"

His mouth drops a little. "I certainly didn't intend to infer—"

"From what my cousin told me, she was upstairs in her room asleep when she was awakened by noises. Thinking I had arrived early, she was about to get out of bed when the door opened and two masked men rushed in. That's all she remembers."

Chief Zandt raises his eyebrows, as if my explanation seems a little too far-fetched.

"Was she bound when you found her?" he asked.

I hesitate for a second, then say. "I guess you could call it that. Any kid might have done a better job. Still it's pretty obvious she's been given some sort of drug."

He eyes Arlene for a few seconds then says, "Yeah. She's on some sort of drug, but whether or not it was given to her against her will..." His shrug underlines its intended message.

Annoyed at his implication, I steal a glance at Arlene, who doesn't even seem to notice. I'm still trying to think of an adequate comeback when Chief Zandt begins to speak into the microphone on his shoulder. In minutes we hear footsteps on the wooden steps rising from the water's edge.

Two uniforms, one holding the roll of bright yellow police line tape, appear on the deck and Zandt motions them over. "Can you show us where Miss Armington saw the two masked men?"

After directing the men to the living room and then on to Arlene's room upstairs at the end of the hall, I return to the kitchen.

When I enter, the chief stands and says, "They'll be dusting the living room as well as the room upstairs for prints. I suggest you two find yourselves a place to stay in town until that part of the investigation is wrapped up. I'll need your cell number so I can advise you of our progress."

After he takes out his cell and enters the number I give him, I say, "I haven't been here in fifteen years. Could you give me a few suggestions about where to stay?"

He thinks a minute. "First place comes to mind is The Woods Inn. It's right down the road and has a restaurant and a pretty good bar if I remember correctly."

He starts to go, then says, "Might want to take a jacket. Front's coming through. Typical. Enjoy."

CHAPTER 3

The sky has filled with heavy, dark clouds and a cold wind rushes through the open window over the sink. After I batten down the kitchen, I manage to get a fleece jacket on Arlene and load her and our luggage into my rental.

I check my watch. Almost seven. Even though the EMT gave Arlene a "pass," I should probably get a second opinion. Then I remember the Central Adirondack Family Practice in Old Forge closes at four, and the closest twenty-four-hour ER is in Utica.

I give Arlene a broad smile. "How are you doing, Cuz?"

Her eyes fill. "How the hell do you think I'm doing, Cuz? Let's just get out of here. Okay?"

Even though she's just lost her mother, I'm startled by Arlene's sudden sarcasm. My cousin and I have been buddies since the playpen. In fact she's more like a sister to me than my own.

The trip to The Woods Inn is thankfully short and once we're settled in our room, I check my cell.

Great reception, but there's Arlene to consider. Even though she seems to have sobered up a bit, she's in no shape to handle anything except putting one foot in front of the other.

I decide that telling Arlene a little white lie won't be too awful if she catches me in it. "Hey, Cuz, I need to make a few calls, but there doesn't seem to be any reception in here. Will you be all right if I leave you alone for a few?"

Arlene doesn't seem to hear me. She's sitting cross-legged on her bed, fixating on her arms. First she frenziedly scratches her left arm with her right hand, and then reverses the operation.

"What on earth are you doing?"

She continues to scratch. "Damn bugs."

I open the door. "I'll be right out here in the hall. Okay, Arlene?"

She nods, then returns to the scratching.

∞⨯∞

I'm relieved my mother doesn't answer the phone. It's always a hassle to get past her litany of small complaints. According to her, the only bright lights in her dreary life are Angela and D-3 (our family nickname for Duncan the third) and how excited she is about the news of a second grandchild.

Dad's soft hello brings my first tears since the tragedy.

"What's wrong, Allie?"

"Oh, Dad, I don't even know where to begin." I take a few breaths, finally manage to stop the tears, and then let the truth tumble forward.

"It's Aunt Sallie. She's dead. Murdered. At least that's how it looks."

His sharp gasp is followed by, "Oh, Allie, how awful for you." After a brief silence he says, "Arlene?"

"Arlene is with me. I found her tied up on the bed in our room at the cottage. She's definitely not well, but there isn't a hospital for miles. I'm pretty sure whoever killed Aunt Sallie must have drugged Arlene too."

Then the tears win out and I sob. "It's a freaking mess, Dad. You'll have to tell Uncle Aiden. I just can't do it. I just can't."

"Of course, I'll call him. Don't give it another thought. I'll call you back as soon as I get in touch with Aiden."

I hang up and go back to the room.

Arlene is still scratching.

"I talked to my dad. He's calling yours."

She jerks her head up. "Oh my God! Dad! I didn't even think about him." She stares into space for a few seconds, then returns to her scratching.

It's like talking to a zombie whose mind checks in for short periods, then wanders away. "Don't worry, my dad's taking care of things in Wilmette."

The scratching grows faster with each word I speak. Finally, I can't stand it anymore. "Look, Arlene, if you don't stop that, you won't have any skin left."

Her eyes fill. "I caaan't. They won't go away until—until . . ." Then her mouth clamps shut.

Then I realize she's close to hysteria and quickly change the subject. "I'm starving, aren't you? How about we hit the dining room before I pass out from hunger?"

Arlene stops scratching for only a second to say, "I'm not even a little hungry. But you go. I'd like to try to get some sleep."

I shrug. My cousin's back at the scratching again. No point in pressing the issue. "Okay. But I can't believe you're not hungry because I'm famished. I'll be downstairs if you need me."

I'm just entering the lobby area when my cell vibrates. Dad. "Did you find him?"

"Poor Aiden. Fortunately he was at Ardythe's for dinner and will stay the night. Thank heaven he won't be alone. How's Arlene holding up?"

"As well as can be expected."

"Brother told me he and Ardythe will take the first flight out of O'Hare tomorrow and rent a car in Syracuse." He pauses, then offers, "Do you want me to come? If you need me, I can be on the next plane."

My eyes mist. My dad is Mr. Ever Faithful. Call him and he's there. What a guy.

"Of course, I want you to come, but don't. If Ardythe and Arlene are here, I'd like to step out of the way and be available only when they need me. Uncle Aiden will need you later."

My dad's soft response conveys his love and support. "I know you'll take care of the things that need to be done up there. See you in Wilmette."

After we trade goodbyes, I head for the dining room and order the beet salad and the meatloaf with a side of garlic "smashed" potatoes. The food is surprisingly tasty and, along with a couple of glasses of wine, smoothes out my anxiety just a bit.

I head back to the room to give Arlene the news, but even as I put my key card in the slot, I know the truth before I even open the door. Arlene is gone.

I race to the lobby for help, but no one is at the desk. It's then I realize I left the keys to my rental in the room. Panicked, I hurry to the parking lot. My rental is gone.

Arlene has escaped, and I have absolutely no clue where to begin my search.

I punch in Chief Zandt's cell and when he answers, I blurt out the necessary details. "Is Arlene with you at the cottage?"

"Can't answer that. I'm at home. Dinner, you know. But I can check with forensics and get back to you."

I thank him and sign off to pace the lobby until my cell vibrates.

Zandt has bad news. No Arlene. But his next bits of information fill in some of the blanks. "Forensics is done and the body has been taken to St. Elizabeth's Hospital in Utica for the autopsy. FYI, the coroner's estimate on the time of death is between ten a.m. and one o'clock. And oh yeah, you're free to return to the house if you want."

It's doubtful that Arlene would go back to the cottage under the circumstances, and I'm not interested in doing that at all. The thought of sleeping alone at a murder site doesn't sound like it would be too smart.

"Guess I'll stay put tonight since I already own the room. But first, I have to find Arlene."

The chief lets out a long breath. "I'd give it up for tonight, Miss Armington. I don't have the manpower to assist your search in the dark. I'd advise you to stay put so she can find you."

"But what about those men? What if they come back?"

"My best guess is they're long gone. They'd have to be brain-dead to come back to the scene of the crime."

"Did forensics find anything?"

He snorts. "If you mean evidence, not much. There were no fingerprints. If what your cousin says is true, the men wore gloves as well as ski masks. But the coroner determined that the probable cause of death resulted from drowning. Of course we can't say for sure until the autopsy is completed, but it seems like this could be a tragic yet simple suicide."

I'm too shocked to speak. I'd had my doubts about a small-town forensics team, but this? This is unthinkable.

"Miss Armington?" The chief's voice sounds like it's coming from the bottom of a well. "Did we lose connection?"

"I'm still here," I say, my voice low. I choose my words carefully, trying not to let my anger get the best of me. "Your forensics team can't be serious about suicide. My cousin was attacked and my aunt murdered within minutes of each other. Do they honestly think Sallie drowned herself?"

"Hold your horses. Like I said, we won't know anything for sure until we get the autopsy results. And forensics is doing the best they can. But let's face it: We don't get many situations like this up here. I've only been on one murder in the last twenty years."

Zandt's words are hardly reassuring. He doesn't seem at all alarmed or concerned. Shouldn't the fact that murders don't happen very often make this case a priority? And suddenly, I can't help but wonder: Has the chief been compromised?

"Thanks for your time," I tell him, eager to get off the phone.

I return to the hotel room and, too tired to floss or brush, I throw myself fully clothed beneath the comforter and fall into a dreamless sleep.

CHAPTER 4

When dawn comes, I shower and change into a fresh outfit. In the lobby there's a table laden with goodies for early-risers, so I chow down a couple of bear claws and a mug of free coffee before securing a ride back to Hotanawa.

I'm not sure why I'm returning to the scene of an unsolved crime. Maybe because a part of me is hoping Arlene will be there—that she went back to the last place she saw her mother alive.

To my disappointment the rental car isn't in the parking area but Aunt Sallie's Toyota is standing in its customary spot. At least now I'll have wheels.

As I recall, the keys should be in the usual spot—under the back-seat floor mat on the driver's side.

I seriously consider checking out the cottage. Then I think, *Damn! Have I lost it already?* Is returning to the scene of the crime, when there's a murderer on the loose, the most intelligent move? But on the other hand I've got lots of questions, and if Chief Zandt isn't going to answer them, I'll have to find another way.

It's freezing in the kitchen so I turn on the oven and start the coffee before taking a tour through the downstairs rooms.

The forensics team has left everything pretty much as I remember: the overturned chair, opened drawers with their contents strewn across the Navajo rug. How could anyone think this was a suicide? Something is definitely fishy.

I gather the papers, right the desk chair and shut the drawers, then return to the kitchen, which is starting to get nice and toasty. It's then I take time to sip a mug of coffee and go over what happened the day before.

So many questions to consider: First, since Hotanawa and its whereabouts are virtually unknown to outsiders, why did those men chose Holden Cottage? It's not the first structure one sees when driving through the main gate into the compound. In fact, if a person didn't know where it was, the cottage would be missed altogether.

Even stranger, the cottage contains nothing of value except for a few pieces of furniture from the Victorian era, the main one being the inlaid commode, once lovely, but now with a peeling veneer and stained marble top; two Victorian side tables; a couple of fake Tiffany lamps; and finally, a very worn Navajo rug—hardly enough to kill for.

So, why kill Aunt Sallie? Had she seen something she shouldn't? Run across something illicit?

Or what if Arlene is fabricating her story? I hate the thought of doubting my cousin and one of my oldest friends, but her behavior since the murder has been pretty suspicious. Less than twenty-four hours after her mother's death, she's vanished. What if Chief Zandt is right and there were never any men with ski masks at all? What if the whole thing was staged?

I feel a prickly fear at the back of my neck, wondering just what Arlene has gotten herself into. I look over my shoulder, suddenly conscious that I'm alone at the scene of a murder. It's then I notice a long sheet of paper on the floor between the kitchen table and the wall and lean down to retrieve what turns out to be Aunt Sallie's grocery list. My heart flutters. She never made it to the Big M.

Suddenly eager to get out of the uncomfortably quiet cottage, I grab the list and don a large fleece jacket hanging on a row of pegs in the workshop next to the Toyota keys. "Alan Armington" is written on the label inside. I wrap it around my body and let his familiar scent saturate my nostrils. It almost makes him seem here.

Since I have no brothers, Alan often filled that vacancy. He was the one who warned me away from Fin after I told him about that first kiss at the fountain.

"You better watch out for him, Allie. He's no good," Alan had said in that sober way of his. "He'd rather cheat than play it straight and his old man encourages it."

At the top of the stone steps I pause and look down the drive. I know the other cottages and the boathouse are locked, but it's been fifteen years since I was last here and curiosity wins. Besides, maybe I'll find some clue as to Arlene's whereabouts. I know this is wishful thinking, but I head for the main part of the compound anyway.

All of the cottages have identical floor plans. Since they were built only for summer use, there's no heat except from a large fireplace in the living room or the oven in the kitchen.

Upstairs, on either side of a wide hall that opens onto a sleeping porch above the kitchen, are four bedrooms with a bath in between each two.

With unusual foresight for the early 1900s, off the living room of each cottage is a one-story master bedroom and bath separated by a small covered walkway.

And at water's edge sits the *pièce de résistance*, the rambling three-story boathouse that serves as the compound's social gathering spot.

Six boat slips hold two vintage Gar Woods, one Chris-Craft, and two Sunfish sailboats.

There are also two outboard skiffs used for trips up the lake to Inlet for a burger, or to one of the many small islands for a picnic, or to a neighbor's dock to sunbathe.

Above the slips is a large living and dining area with a professional kitchen and an attached commercial laundry. On the floor above that is the staff quarters.

If I recall correctly, there were usually five on staff: two cooks, two dock boys who also served as waiters for the evening meal, and of course, Frederick Ashton, the compound's general manager, who saw to everything from meals to laundry.

Still, times are different now. I'm sure the staff and routines have changed. It doesn't matter. I won't be around when the season cranks up the first of July. But I can't help but wonder what will happen when news of Sallie's murder reaches the other families. Will it destroy Hotanawa's reputation as a perfect Eden?

I've just started down the path to the boathouse when I hear something moving in the trees to my left. I turn in the direction of the noise but I can see little through the stands of beech and hemlock that separate the compound from the adjoining property—Findlay Holden's property.

Uncle Findlay's sons, Fin and Emery, summered on the several acres abutting the eastern boundary of Hotanawa compound.

Fin was a hunk, with coal-black hair and Sinatra's blue eyes. I last saw him the summer before he was to enter Cornell.

Emery, as blond as his brother was dark, was a year younger and looking at Dartmouth.

Both young men, tall, lithe, and handsome, were Sallie's cousins but easily could have been her children. Her Uncle Findlay had been a menopause baby and a very unwelcome surprise for everyone in the Holden family.

I hear the sound again, only this time it's not so close. I realize with a start that no one in the world knows where I am. If I were to disappear, no one would know where to look.

I walk cautiously to the edge of the woods.

Fifteen years ago one could easily make out the outline of the Findlay Holden home through the trees. Now the woods have grown thick—so thick that the narrow path the Holden children once made between their house and the compound has all but disappeared.

I stand still and listen. What is it I heard? Or is it only that I *want* to hear something—something that will answer all my unanswered questions?

After a few minutes of only the wind echoing through the leaves, I push away an involuntary shiver and head back across the compound to the Toyota.

CHAPTER 5

The trip to the Big M in Eagle Bay brings another rush of nostalgia. For half an hour, I focus on filling the cart, trying not to think about anything. But there's one item on the grocery list, the very last one, that's illegible. I squint hard, trying to read it. Something about the way it's written, the obviously hurried scrawl, sends a shiver down my spine.

I tell myself not to make an issue out of nothing, and to forget about the last item. It doesn't take me long to get the rest of the groceries on the list, and I'm back in the kitchen of Holden Cottage before an hour has passed, unable to think about anything besides my aunt's death and my cousin's disappearance.

I've just put the last grocery sack on the counter, and poured another mug of coffee to chase away the chill, when I hear tires crunching on the gravel driveway, followed by a door slam and footfall on the stone steps.

It's Arlene, face red and splotchy, with eyes so puffy they're almost sealed shut.

"Where in hell have you been?"

She tries a timid smile. "Sorry. I just had to get out of there. The itching was driving me nuts."

I notice she isn't scratching, but I'm still furious with her. "That's not going to do it for me. I was frantic. I even called Chief Zandt."

She shrugs and then begins to unpack the groceries. After the canned goods are stowed in the pantry, she looks into my glower and gives me a pleading look. "I said I was sorry. Don't worry. I—I slept in the car in front of the Inlet Police Station."

When I say, "Ohhh? Really?" she looks away, then starts folding the empty sacks.

I watch her jerky movements in fascination. As I recall, Arlene was never much for frenzy. In fact, when we were younger, we used to call her "slo-mo."

Then it dawns on me. She has to be taking some sort of weight-loss pills. That's what's hyping her up.

"Your dad and Ardythe will be here in time for dinner. What about Alan?"

"He probably won't come."

"Of course he'll come. Why wouldn't he?"

"I thought you knew."

My mind flies in all directions. Alan was his mother's pride and joy: cum laude from Princeton, Baker Scholar at Harvard Business School; surely nothing had gone awry between those two.

At my tentative, "Knew what?" Arlene says, "Alan's bank sent him to Hong Kong along with Virginia, the kids, the nanny, and the dog." She sighs. "Of course he'll want to come back for the funeral, but I don't know about the rest of his family. It's such a long trip. Thank heavens Ardythe likes to take charge of things."

Her eyes fill once again as she dabs her nose with a tissue. "I just can't believe it. Why were those men at the cottage? It's all just so strange."

Her voice dies to a whisper as she fitfully tears the tissue into shreds, then rolls them into tiny pills which she carefully lines up in rows on the table.

This is not the Arlene I knew. Even though she had been a little on the plump side for most of her adult life, she didn't seem to mind. She was always the cool gal, and funny too, and so bright.

The butter streusel coffee cake, a Holden Cottage breakfast tradition, now sits in the open space between the half-unloaded grocery sacks so both Arlene and I can get to it.

Memories of those delicious coffee cakes shared at Holden Cottage flood my brain, causing me to make an absolute pig of myself. I notice Arlene has merely picked at the one slender sliver on her plate and is now rapidly stabbing the leftover crust with her fork.

She looks up, eyes accusing. "Why are you staring at me?"

"Was I staring? I didn't mean to. It's just that I can't forget how much we both loved butter streusel."

Arlene tries a smile and shakes her head. "Sorry. I guess I'm just a little jumpy. It's all so unsettling. Complete strangers in our home. Why? Why were they here?"

She shakes her head, looks down at her sweater, then concentrates for the next few minutes on removing all the wooly pills from the front. Then she must remember I'm in the room, because she jerks her head up and says, "How was the Big M?"

I shrug. "Not at all crowded, but the shelves are well-stocked. I found everything except for . . ."

I pull the list from my pocket and shove it past the coffee cake. "What do you think that last item is?"

She takes it and studies it for a few seconds. "That doesn't look like Momma's writing. Momma's a neat freak. If she makes—*made*—a mistake, she would copy that list again."

She shoves the list across the table to me and mumbles, "It looks like it could be 'fish' but we never buy fish up here. Big M carries only frozen fish and Momma hates frozen anything." At that, she bursts into tears and cradles her head in her arms.

The wall phone in the back hall rings, startling both of us to our feet. Arlene slumps back into her chair as I edge past her to get it on the third ring.

It's my father. "Aiden just called. They're stopping in Utica before they come up. How's Arlene?"

"Not so good."

"He'll notify me when they decide about the funeral."

There's only the briefest pause before Dad adds, "If I know Aiden, that's it for Hotanawa. The place went to Sallie after her brothers were killed, but she was never really considered a Holden. Thanks to that rat bastard Uncle Fin, the Armingtons were never treated as equals by the three other families. Aiden hated that. If you remember he called them the 'Tanawas' since there were no longer any Holdens left besides Sallie."

I can't believe my father's grim pronouncement. Both our families had had such fun together on Fourth Lake. I try to remember any unpleasantness between our family and the others; none comes. But then, we were kids.

My father's soft voice breaks into my thoughts.

"Just know I'm thinking of you . . . and your mother and Angela send their love as well."

My sister is newly pregnant with her second child and unable to travel. I can easily buy Angela's concern about how I'm holding up, but I know full well that Dad has ad-libbed Mother's interest in my well-being.

I hear the soft click that means another call is waiting.

"Thanks, Dad," I say, "I've got to go." We hang up and I click over. "Hello?"

"Arlene?"

"No. This is Alice Armington speaking. Who is this?"

There's a pause.

"Allie? How nice to hear your voice after all this time. It's Clarissa Napier. Well, Clarissa Demme now. Remember me?"

Of course I remember. Clarissa, who is a couple of years younger than I, was a stuck-up kid who made it a point to tell all the other kids that even though her family lived in Winnetka, she was a Napier of the Nantucket Napiers who arrived on the second or third wave of New World settlers.

She must have heard about Sallie and is worried there could be a murderer on the loose at Hotanawa. But if I remember Clarissa, she's pretending to call to offer her condolences when info is all she wants.

I do my best to sounds appreciative. "Of course. It's very kind of you to call, Clarissa."

"Think nothing of it. I just heard about Sallie and I can't believe it. She was such a lovely woman, with so much to live for. What could possibly possess her to go and do a thing like this?"

"A thing like ..." My voice trails off as I realize what Clarissa is saying. She isn't calling because she thinks there's been a murder: She's calling to confirm the suicide.

"Clarissa," I begin, trying to keep the indignation out of my voice, "I don't know what you've been told, but—"

She talks over my next word. "Oh, you poor, poor dears, you must be wracked with grief. Don't bother with the details, I know the whole story because I just spoke to Bo, or as you probably know him, Chief Zandt. His family has a lovely camp on the South Shore Road. What a tragedy for everyone. Though I must say, the other families are relieved it wasn't anything violent."

When she pauses to take a breath, I try again. "Clarissa, if you'll just let me—"

"Can you imagine the media frenzy that would descend on Hotanawa if there'd been a murder? I shudder to think of the *Chicago Trib*'s field day at everybody's expense. And worse still, our little slice of paradise would be ruined forever. We would never have any peace!"

I am so angry I can't find my voice. Clarissa has some nerve!

And then I realize exactly who compromised Chief Zandt: the other families of Hotanawa. Boy, was that quick!

Clarissa's next words override my thoughts. "Please accept the Napier family's sincere condolences. I suppose we'll see you at the funeral since we won't be out there until right before July Fourth. No one in their right mind comes to Fourth Lake this time of year."

I force my response through clenched teeth. "Thank you, Clarissa, dear. I'll convey your condolences to the Armingtons."

After a too-long pause, Clarissa asks, "Do you know when the funeral will be?"

"No date has been set." I want to scream, *Sallie's only been dead one day!* But all I can blurt out is, "Thanks so much for calling," and abruptly hang up.

It all makes so much sense. Somehow the other families have put pressure on the police to shelve their investigation of Sallie's murder. God forbid the reputation of their perfect little vacation spot be muddied by a violent crime and bruited about in the papers.

I don't know what kind of incentive the families might have offered Zandt, but with the kind of money they have access to, I wouldn't be at all surprised if Sallie's case has been carefully filed away as a suicide for a couple new cop cars or putting together a forensics team that might actually do their job.

I sigh, wondering just how far the rot might go? All the way to Herkimer? They say a fish rots from the head down.

No matter. If the proper authorities aren't going to get involved, that means it's up to me. There's no way I'm going to let this case go unsolved. My main "gig" is to find who murdered Aunt Sallie. As soon as things settle down, I have every intention of bringing whoever committed this heinous act to their knees.

CHAPTER 6

It's dusk when a weary Uncle Aiden and Arlene's elder sister Ardythe arrive.

Unlike my father who, though tall, is slender and still blond, Aiden is a big strapping man with iron-gray hair.

The two sisters hug as Ardythe murmurs, "Sis, oh, Sis." And Arlene coos, "Ardie, I'm so glad you're here," as both turn to embrace their father.

I murmur the necessary condolences to their backs and leave the three by the fire in the living room. In the kitchen, I begin preparing dinner. As I do, I make a mental list of suspects. Sad to say, the list isn't very long.

Arlene knows more than she's telling. But what is it? And why is she keeping secrets?

My first job is to find out exactly how fatal those secrets are.

❧

I'm almost finished with the dinner prep when Ardythe brings me a glass of Merlot and settles at the kitchen table to nurse hers.

She lets out a long sigh, then says, "I took Arlene upstairs for a nap. She seems so strung out and too damned thin if you ask me."

"How's Uncle Aiden?"

She sadly shakes her head. "Poor Dad. I made him a stiff drink, but he's still just barely operational. You should have seen him at the hospital after he saw Momma's body. Moved like a zombie. I had to drive. Didn't say a word until we walked in the door and saw you and Sis."

I turn away from the stove to settle across the table from her. "How are you holding up?"

She shrugs. "Guess I'm in denial too. It's just so hard to comprehend—I mean the violent nature of Momma's death. Everybody loves—" She takes a deep breath. "Everybody loved Momma."

I can't bear to tell her about the call from Clarissa and the sad truth that the other families, and even the authorities, are dead set on making this look like a suicide. Ardythe is in enough pain; I don't need to add insult to injury.

Tears well and she swallows a couple of times. "Alan was in such shock he couldn't even speak. Virginia had to do the talking for him. You know Momma and he were so close ..." Her voice trails to a whisper. "He was her favorite."

I reach across to pat Ardythe's hand. "As far as I could tell, your mother never showed any favoritism toward any one of you. Unlike my mother, who has never made a secret of doting on Angela. She still does."

I take a sip of wine and change the subject. "I was surprised to see that Arlene has lost so much weight."

Ardythe stares at me for a few seconds before she replies. "I haven't seen Sis since Christmas. The change is, to say the least, quite a shock."

When I nod my agreement, Ardythe leans forward and lowers her voice. "I think there's someone new in her life."

"Oh?"

She lets out a long breath. "After Sis broke up with that guy at Dennison, she didn't date. Not anybody. We were so worried that she might not ever ..." Her voice trails as she studies the bottom of her wine glass.

"Have you met him?"

"No. None of us has. I think Sis planned to introduce him to Momma and you first."

Ardythe's next words are a shock. "Did you know Sis took an indefinite leave of absence from the Chicago Board of Trade and has been living up here since just after New Year's?"

I barely hide my shock. "That's news to me."

Ardythe's brow wrinkles. "I thought you two talked on a weekly basis."

"No. Not lately. Though she invited me last Thanksgiving when you were in Houston. But I only spoke with Arlene once in March and that was to discuss the change of date for my visit."

Ardythe lets out a prolonged sigh. "We don't know what to think. After all, Sis is thirty-six. And because she's been a really insightful trader, she's put away plenty of money—enough to purchase a good-sized apartment on Elm down in the city. That's why it's so hard to understand what drew her up here—unless it's a man."

Now that I think about it, it is sort of strange that Arlene never once mentioned her move from Chicago. Still, in my cousin's defense, Aunt Sallie's sudden and dreadful death has been the main focus of all our conversations.

When I rise to take the salad makings out of the refrigerator, Ardythe says, "Need any help?"

I shake my head, place them on the cutting board, and pick up the knife. "It's sort of a one-woman job. Besides, I like to chop and peel. It helps me think."

Ardythe sighs, "I don't want to think. Not yet, anyway. At least not about what went on here."

She takes a sip of the wine and looks around the kitchen. "Even though I haven't been up here in a long time, I often have vivid dreams about this place."

Ardythe looks up at the ceiling and then smiles for the first time since she arrived. "Remember those dinners? I loved joining the grownups when I was little. And after dinner, the music blaring? Those funny eight-track tapes? Remember 'Here Comes the Sun'? 'Classical Gas'?"

I nod as I replay a memory or two of my own. The sun setting to the west. A stiff breeze from the lake below sways the wrought-iron chandeliers hanging above the family tables in the dining room.

After everyone was settled at their assigned tables, the kitchen doors would swing wide and dinner entered, carried on trays and served family-style.

My favorite night was Thursday—country-fried chicken with mashed potatoes and gravy. Friday was seafood night—with live Maine Lobster flown in by seaplane that morning. And Saturday—a cookout on the boathouse deck, weather permitting, followed by dancing under the stars.

July began with a bang on the Fourth and then was relatively quiet except on weekends, but by early August Hotanawa was in full swing with the cottages bursting at the seams. Visiting kids were in sleeping bags on the porches, their parents in the four bedrooms upstairs.

Every evening after dinner, the different families indulged in a heated competition of charades in front of the massive stone fireplace. A coveted silver trophy was awarded to the family with the most points on Labor Day.

Only Holden Cottage was quiet. After Mom and Dad left for Lampasas, Arlene, Angela, and I were given our own bedrooms. Uncle Aiden and Aunt Sallie were in the master bedroom off the living room. It was just the five of us. By that time Ardythe and Alan had left the compound for other venues.

Ardythe breaks into my reverie. "It's really strange to be up here this time of year. The trees are that wonderful shade of new green and the ferns just unfurled."

"Yeah. It's all new to me too. Our family came when summer was in full bloom. But then you and Alan were seldom here after you both were in high school. Why was that?"

"Mainly because there weren't any kids our age except for Frankie Napier, but he was sent off to camp and stayed on to be a counselor. There weren't any girls even close to my age except for Angela, and she seemed a little too young for me."

Hearing Frankie Napier's name makes me think of his tactless little sister, and I feel sick to my stomach.

"To be honest," I say, "your dad never seemed to care much for this place."

Ardythe nods. "That's true. If your family hadn't visited, I doubt Dad would have made the effort. Still, Momma loved it so much, and he never could refuse her.

"Truth is Dad never forgave Uncle Findlay and the 'Natawas' for saying such hurtful things to Momma when she inherited the cottage.

"And poor Momma felt it worse than any of us. For some reason, even though the other families supported the move because Uncle Fin was such a mean bastard, she often remarked that things never seemed quite the same."

Ardythe shoves up the sleeve on her left arm to reveal a round purple scar. "I hated the spiders. This was from a brown recluse. I almost died. Remember? I know you were here because you were the brave one. You came to my room and put hot compresses on the bite."

"I do remember that summer. Your parents were so worried."

"That's when I began spending the summers at Lake Geneva with mother's best friend Georgie." Her eyes fill. "Oh, dear, I'll have to tell Georgie about Momma. Poor Georgie. They were close as sisters, you know."

I finish slicing the zucchini, then concentrate on finely chopping a small red onion before asking, "Do you know where Arlene's been staying up here?"

Ardythe looks up. "Can't say that I do. Obviously not here." She shivers and draws her sweater closer. "I haven't spoken with Sis since Christmas day."

"That's not unusual, is it? I mean, you two have never been very close."

"True, but we got into a big squabble when we were in the kitchen at Momma's putting together the Waldorf salad. That's when Sis began asking me all sorts of questions about Holden Cottage. I answered as best as I could, but then she asked who would inherit.

"I said, 'Alan, of course. He's the only male heir.' Then Sis said if that were so, Holden Cottage should have gone to Uncle Findlay, not Momma.

"I took umbrage at that. Findlay Holden didn't deserve the cottage. Besides, the other three families hated him. I couldn't believe she was taking up for that rotten old man, so I told her as much and left the kitchen in a huff."

Ardythe shrugs. "Looks like from the way she welcomed me this afternoon, Sis has forgotten all about it. And I'm grateful for that."

She drains her wine glass. "I think I'll get another bottle."

"Don't open one on my account; I can make do with this glass."

Ardythe gives me a trembling smile. "But I can't."

CHAPTER 7

Though it's only just past eight, the three Armingtons are in bed.

Dinner was a somber affair accompanied by stilted discussions about the weather and a few comments about the imminent arrival of the black flies. The conversation lurched along, each sentence punctuated with flatware squeaking on china.

Finally, Uncle Aiden shoved the food around his plate one more time then said, "They called from Utica to say they're done with the autopsy and we can take Sallie home tomorrow."

I raised my head. Uncle Aiden had finally faced the grim and tragic fact that his wife was dead. Arlene and Ardythe's eyes were tear-filled, and then my own tears rose.

Not a word was said until Aiden cleared his throat a couple of times. "I spoke with Alan before we left Chicago. He suggests we Med jet Sallie to the airport near Wilmette."

He looked at each one of us, then pronounced, "We'll leave tomorrow as soon things can be arranged."

"What about the Toyota?" I asked. "You don't want to leave it here. Do you?"

Uncle Aiden's eyes misted and he slowly shook his head. "Of course not. It's just hard to think of everything."

I reached across the table to pat his hand. "Not to worry. Arlene and I will drive the Toyota back to Wilmette. We'll drop off my rental at the Syracuse airport, spend the night there, and drive on to Chicago the next day. How does that sound?"

Arlene remained mute during the entire exchange while her eyes carefully avoided mine.

At those words, she finally spoke up. "No. No. I want to ride with you, Dad. I wouldn't be any good driving to Syracuse alone. I'm just too scattered at this point to drive anything. Let Ardythe and Allie take care of the cars."

Ardythe shook her head. "I'm sorry, Dad, but spending a night in Syracuse just won't work for me. I have to get back to Chicago by tomorrow afternoon at the latest." She glanced at her watch. "I'm hoping I could accompany Momma on the jet."

Aiden whirled to face his eldest daughter. "No way in hell. I need you in Utica."

"But can't Sis and Allie help? Doug and I are hosting—"

"Hosting? The hell with you and your gee-dee social events. For Pete's sake, Ardie, we're in the middle of a family crisis here. Your mother has just been brutally murdered and the whole town's crazy enough to think she did it to herself. We have to get the body back to Chicago for burial. You'll just have to cancel your plans and that's that."

Ardythe paled at his onslaught, then she lowered her eyes. "Of course, Dad. You're right. I'll do whatever you want."

He abruptly stood. "I want to leave here by noon at the latest and I expect you all to be ready."

∽⋈∾

I'm settled on the deck in an Adirondack chair, wrapped in the heavy fleece jacket that belongs to Alan, holding the last glass of the third bottle of Merlot.

As I replay the events, I spot a few discrepancies in Arlene's story that I didn't quite pick up on at first. She said there were two men in masks, but forensics found no other fingerprints except Sallie's and Arlene's. Of course, I can't say I really trust the same team that ruled Sallie's death as an official suicide. And as the chief said, if there *were* masked men, they were probably wearing gloves, but Arlene didn't say anything about gloves.

And if Arlene has been up here since just after New Year's, where has she been staying?

She couldn't have stayed at Holden Cottage. Like all of the other buildings in the compound, it isn't winterized.

When I put down my wine to draw the fleece more tightly about me, I notice lights filtering through the woods that separate Hotanawa from the Findlay Holden house.

I peer through the darkness, almost positive that there were no lights on when I first came out to the deck because I would have noticed.

Grateful that I didn't turn on the deck lights, I focus all my attention on the house through the woods. I know from my conversation with Clarissa that the other families aren't here yet, and won't be for weeks. So who is it? And what are they doing?

I begin to make a plan. I'll get up early, reconnoiter the other Holdens' house, then return to the cottage in plenty of time to help pack the Toyota.

It seems like a good plan. Just a little stroll. No confrontations. Just take a peek and then come right back.

When my eyelids begin to droop and a yawn rises, I realize it's time to give up the surveillance and head for bed.

CHAPTER 8

The day is just breaking when I reach the edge of the woods separating the Hotanawa compound from the other Holden camp. The frigid dawn air seeps through my fleece and chills me to the bone—though I'm not sure that's the only reason I'm shivering.

What am I doing? I want to find out why there were lights in the woods last night, but am I being crazy by wandering around alone mere days after my aunt was murdered?

And if the Napiers and the other families are determined to keep it quiet, it might mean they have something to hide.

I don't know exactly what I'm looking for, but my gut tells me I'll know it when I find it. So I keep walking.

It isn't hard to find traces of the old path, but fifteen years of thick undergrowth presents a big problem.

After struggling through the low plants and sliding around the leaning, spindly pine trunks, I see broken branches and crushed brush ahead.

The sounds I heard yesterday weren't made by a deer. Someone was in these woods. And whoever it was must have seen me. I suppress a rising shiver, then automatically reach for my Beretta tucked in the right pocket of Alan's fleece.

With each step I take, a prickly sense of unease grows as I realize that once I come out of the woods, I will have to cross almost forty yards without any cover. It's then I pause to check out my options and then make a judgment call. I quickly retrace my steps until I'm out of the woods.

I climb the Hotanawa driveway to Route 28 in a matter of minutes, despite the fact that the hill, that once seemed an easy upward hike, now seems much steeper.

I pause at the entrance to catch my breath before turning right to walk along the highway. Several hundred yards down the road, the entrance to the Findlay Holden property is marked by two columns, not unlike the pair bracketing the drive into "Hotanawa."

That's where the similarity ends. Once the road passes beneath the umbrella of dense evergreens at the top of the drive, it crosses an open field. No trees have been planted to shield the property from prying eyes. There's no formal landscaping at all, just wild grass and weeds that have sprung up with the warmer weather and in dire need of a mowing.

Unlike the cluster of homes at Hotanawa, the main house on this property is situated on the far left side of the open field with its outlying buildings placed discreetly behind it. Behind those buildings the forest begins.

All the buildings are painted in a pale yellow. The central house is two stories, with a wraparound porch.

I walk up the drive past the wheelchair ramps leading to the front and back porches, and peek through the garage door windows.

Aunt Sallie's silver Toyota is parked inside next to a dark green van.

Arlene is here and she's not alone.

But, when did she leave the compound?

I'm a light sleeper. I should have heard the engine fire since the car was parked just across the drive.

My first instinct is to enter the house, but then red flags start to wave. I have no idea about the interior layout or the number of people inside. It's best to wait until I'm back on safer ground.

After checking my trusty Beretta, I sidle down the left side of the garage to stand a moment. I hear traffic. The highway, which makes a curve to the right after the Findlay Holden entrance, must only be a hundred or so yards away.

The wood is the best way out. I weave through the trees, stopping now and then to be sure I'm headed in the right direction, and finally reach Route 28.

Whatever Arlene is doing on Findlay Holden's property, I intend to find out.

CHAPTER 9

It's almost ten by the time I make my way back to Holden Cottage
where Uncle Aiden, Ardythe, and Arlene are seated at the kitchen
table.

I'm not surprised to see Arlene. She had plenty of time to drive up
Fin Holden's driveway and through the gates to Hotanawa while I was
stumbling through the woods.

My uncle jumps up before I can step into the room. "Where in hell
have you been? We've been worried sick."

The look on Ardythe's face echoes her father's concern but Arlene's
eyes are lowered to avoid the question in mine.

I ease out of the jacket, making sure that neither my cell nor my
Beretta is exposed. "I'm so sorry. I didn't mean to complicate things. I
woke early, went for a walk, and lost all track of the time."

Uncle Aiden nods. "Well then, now that you're safely back, we can
get on with everything we have to do before we can leave. You and Sis
clean up while Ardie and I pack the Toyota."

He motions for Ardythe to rise, then says, "The girls will follow
me to the airport where the hearse will meet us. I contacted Med
jet and they're set for a mid-afternoon departure. Ardie and Sis will
spend the night in Syracuse and drive on to Wilmette tomorrow."

"Surely there must be something I can do to help?"

Aiden fishes a key out of his pocket and hands it to me. "It would
be great if you could clean out the fridge and lock up the cottage. No
telling when we'll be coming back—if ever."

"I'll be happy to stay here until you decide about the funeral, then I'll fly into Chicago."

"That would be nice." He gives me a warm smile. "You've always been like a sister to Arlene. Always there for her."

When the two leave the kitchen, Arlene leaps up and grabs the coffee pot. She doesn't look at me, but waves a mug in my direction. "Want a mug before I rinse the pot?"

"Think I'll pass."

I watch as she devotes the next few minutes to frenzied scouring, then re-scouring the coffee pot before putting it back in its place.

Then the sickening realization comes.

I quickly run down the meth-user's checklist of symptoms: extreme weight-loss, paranoia, hyperactivity. Arlene's fits them all. She's in trouble. Deep trouble.

When she starts for the door, I realize she has no intention of talking to me.

"Hold it, Arlene."

"Ardie's waiting."

"She can wait. You and I have to have a little chat."

She shakes her head. "I don't have anything to say."

"But I do. Sit."

She slumps in the chair across from me and lets out a long exasperated breath. "What?"

"Do you have enough to get back to Wilmette?"

"Enough?"

"Don't play dumb with me. I saw Sallie's Toyota in Fin's garage."

"So what? I'm an adult. I can do as I please."

I let out a long sad sigh. "Yes. That's certainly true."

She gives me a triumphant smile. "That's why I asked you to come early. I wanted you and Momma to be the first to know. Fin and I are getting married." Then she lowers her voice. "I had his baby in March."

My mouth drops but she ignores my shock to hurry on.

"Fin and I began seeing each other last summer, but kept it quiet. Then, when I found out I was pregnant, I moved up here."

I do a quick calculation. Fin had worked fast. No way the Holdens would obstruct a marriage if a baby were involved.

I swallow my suspicions and gush, "Oh, Arlene, I'm so happy for you. Where is he—she?"

She looks away. "It's a girl. But I don't know where she is. Fin won't tell me. Says it's for my own good. When he found out I was hooked, he took her back to Chicago."

Arlene sounds as if she's been coached. No emotion, no anguish. Maybe it's the meth, but she hardly acts like a pining mother.

"Does your family know?"

She shakes her head. "Fin thinks we should wait until after the wedding."

What I want to ask is: How can she let her baby be taken from her without putting up a fight? Something is very fishy. Arlene acts like she doesn't care. Maybe that's the problem. Fin needs her involvement to put over the scam.

Or did Sallie somehow find out about the baby and confront Fin? Did he kill her to shut her up?

I can see Arlene's waiting for some sort of response. But it won't be "congratulations," that's for sure.

"So, what's your drug *du jour*?"

"What do you mean?"

"What are you using?" I hopefully add, "Cocaine?"

When she shakes her head my heart falls.

"Oh, Lord, you're not—not *meth*."

She looks down for a few seconds, then her eyes meet mine. "I'm snorting only a few lines a day. Fin wants me thin for the wedding. This is the thinnest I've ever been."

She looks up, eyes hopeful. "Hey, you might want to try some. Best high I've ever had."

"So I hear. But the trouble is, no matter how much you do, you'll never get that same terrific kick."

Her eyes lower as she stammers, "Y-yeah. It isn't the same. And I get so jittery if I don't—"

I finish the sentence. "Have a bump every hour or so? That makes perfect sense to me. You're an addict, Arlene."

"No, no. I am *not* an addict. I can stop whenever I want."

"Sure you can. But then the bugs come, don't they?"

Arlene shakes her head and hugs her arms to her. "They don't if I get a bump before—"

"Before you come all the way down? So I'm asking you again, do you have enough to get back to Wilmette?"

She sighs. "Yes."

"And when you get to Wilmette? What happens then?"

"I'll stop."

"No. You won't because you can't stop on your own. You'll need professional help to detox and stay clean."

When she stands, I motion her back into the chair. "I'm sure you remember that I worked as an assistant DA on a grand jury panel."

Arlene nods. "Vaguely. I was just getting started on the Board of Trade back then."

"That's right. So, from my past experience, do you mind if I ask a few pertinent questions?"

She shrugs. "Whatever."

"Have you bought any meth?"

"No. Fin gives me all I want."

"Sold any?"

She shakes her head.

"Cooked any?"

Arlene gives me an indignant sniff. "Of course not."

"So, at this moment, technically you're just an addict. And maybe you're not so far gone that with the proper rehab you can get back to living the life you left. Raise your daughter. Keep your job."

I pause a minute to let things sink in, hoping that my sensible, funny, acerbic cousin is still in there— somewhere.

"You've been living with Fin since you came up here New Year's and you had his baby in March. Why did he take the baby away?"

"I couldn't breast-feed. Actually, I couldn't do much at all."

"And left you with no drugs?"

She shrugs. "I have a source. No problem."

"Do you have any idea where the baby is? And who's taking care of her?"

She shakes her head. "I told you, I haven't been well. Things are sorta foggy."

"So I'm guessing you moved back to the cottage from Fin's place the day your mother arrived."

Arlene nods and gives me a wry smile. "You could always read me like a book. But my parents have known about Fin and me for some time. Not about the baby, that was going to be the surprise." She looks down and murmurs, "Now everything's gone to hell."

"Boy, is that the understatement of the year."

Arlene raises a cautionary finger. "Just as a heads-up, Fin's not as crippled as we all thought he was."

"What do you mean by that?"

She ignores my question. "Maybe if I say I'll go with you, we could wait to leave until after noon tomorrow. Fin promised to bring me some of the fresh batch they're cooking in the morning."

I stop breathing as those reliable red flags start to wave. Sallie must have stumbled onto something. Or maybe Arlene, high from a bump, had confessed. Didn't she say that she and Sallie had had a big fight their first night together?

I shake my head. "You're father's not going to let you do that. Didn't you hear him?"

Arlene nods, then hunches into her shoulders.

"I know I sound like a broken record, but if you continue to do meth, you'll eventually be forced to buy some on the street. And if you start buying on the street, the law will eventually catch you. Then you'll have a record. And if for some lucky reason they don't slap you in prison, you won't be able to trade. Ever. Your career will be shot to hell."

She shakes away my words. "Fin wouldn't let—"

"Fin's a shit. Don't you get it? All he wants is Holden Cottage. First he got you hooked on meth and then he took your baby away. If you want to save yourself, you have to get away from him. That means you have to go home today. And when you get there, you have to get professional help."

She glares at me, eyes sullen. "Look who thinks she's in charge now."

"I'm only looking out for you, Arlene. Fin is only looking out for himself. He'd do anything to get this place. Even . . ."

I stop myself as Arlene looks at me, eyes wide.

"Even what?"

I sigh.

"I don't know yet. But you can be sure I'm going to find out."

CHAPTER 10

Ardythe gives me a brief hug before climbing into her mother's Toyota where she waits, motor idling, until Uncle Aiden and Arlene get in the rental and start down the hill.

I'm about to turn away when she lowers the window, leans out, and motions me back.

"Okay. What's with Sis?"

"What do you mean?"

"I watched you two last night at dinner and today when you got back from your walk. She never once looked you in the eye."

I shrug.

"Don't play dumb with me, Allie. There's something definitely wrong with my sister and you know what it is."

I guess she must read the reluctance in my eyes because she raises her voice. "Be straight with me. I don't have time to play games."

What have I been thinking? I should have brought Ardythe into the loop the minute I suspected Arlene's addiction. Ardythe will know how and when to break the news to Uncle Aiden.

"Arlene's hooked on crystal meth."

Ardythe's mouth drops. "Whaaa?"

"I knew something was wrong but not exactly what it was until this morning."

She snaps her mouth into a small, hard line, then she mutters, "Gee, thanks a bunch for the early heads-up."

"Sorry, but I only just confronted her while you and Uncle Aiden were packing the Toyota. It was the first chance I had since I got here.

"Arlene tells me she has enough of the drug to make it to Wilmette without coming down, but after that—" I shake my head. "Just don't let her come down before you can get her into a professional situation. You won't be able to handle what might happen if she gets desperate."

And then it hits me—when someone's on meth, they'd do anything for that next bump. It's too horrible to even think about ... but what if Arlene is somehow involved in Sallie's death? What if Chief Zandt was onto something with his initial line of questioning?

"Sweet God in heaven," Ardythe says. "Don't we have enough on our plate already?"

"I'm really sorry. I wish there were something I could do."

She sighs. "There's nothing you can do. I just hope there's something *we* can. Poor Sis. What a mess."

"But there's more."

"How can there be more?"

"She's involved with Fin Holden. He's the one who got her hooked. Not only that, he makes the stuff. Or has people under his control make it for him."

Ardythe jerks back at that news. "And you say she's been with Fin since ...?"

I hesitate to say anything to Ardythe about Arlene's real or imagined pregnancy and the baby. The facts just don't quite jibe. No use in spreading that news, throwing in the proverbial wrench, until I get to the bottom of things.

"Arlene moved in with him New Year's. She tells me he's asked her to marry him."

She stares away, then gives me an emphatic nod. "Don't worry, we'll handle all of this ... somehow."

After raising the window, Ardythe gives me a limp wave, and eases the Toyota down the road to the bottom of the hill.

Ardythe doesn't know the half of it. I'm glad I decided not to burden her with my long list of fears, but as the Toyota disappears from view, I can't help but feel sick to my stomach.

I remember meth users from my time as an assistant DA. Any loyalty they might have had to a family member or lover was obliterated by their need for the drug. If Fin has his hooks into Arlene and she's a real addict, who knows what he might have convinced her to do?

Or, with her help, what he might have done himself.

There's only one thing to do.

I'm going to find Fin Holden.

CHAPTER 11

I need a safe haven to plan my meeting with Fin. Suddenly, with the rest of the family gone, the house feels like the least safe place in the world. That's when I decide to head back to Woods. It's the intelligent move to make.

I pull out my cell, book a room at Woods, open a Diet Coke, and check my office messages.

Though I've only been away from Houston three days, other than those annoying telemarketers, there are none.

That's not good. Because of my Aunt Sallie's murder and the impending funeral, I'll have to be away from my desk much longer than I anticipated.

This definitely will not please my ex-fiancé—and now brother-in-law, Duncan Bruce, Esq.—who offered me office space on the cheap and an affiliation with his burgeoning law firm.

Though Duncan has often referred to my random involvement with murder as "cockamamie," in truth I probably stumbled into those situations because I am basically nosy.

Still, it was Duncan who encouraged me to enroll in an online PI course. When I sneered that online sounded so bogus, he forwarded me three names. I visited each site, studied them carefully, and finally took the plunge.

There was a lot to take in, but I loved every new challenge the course put forward. How did I know my nosiness would become my biggest asset? In only a short three months I had my diploma from the University of Phoenix.

The first case I took as a private investigator was thrown my way by Clayton Bradford, a criminal defense attorney from Albuquerque who came to my rescue when I was hauled in for shooting the sheriff of Taos last fall. I was innocent, but it took quite a bit of effort to find out who was actually the guilty party.

Because Clay had faith in me (despite my admission that I'm mathematically challenged), I was able to follow the paper trail of a prominent businessman in El Paso who cleverly, or so he thought, managed to scam his partners out of over one hundred million dollars.

Face it: Men's minds turn to mush when they are post-coital. Never mind that the guy dumped his poor wife for a pole-dancer in Juarez, but the idiot proceeded to dump bimbo number one for a second bimbette the following month.

Guess he forgot about scorned women and how they talk, and talk, and talk.

The whole exercise was a piece of cake. Not to mention that I had more than a few dinners with the aforementioned Clay Bradford, who just happened to get to El Paso several times while I was there. We definitely have chemistry going, but he's been married a couple of times and is a little snake-bit.

In mid-April Duncan referred me my second client, a wealthy, middle-aged widow whose twice-divorced fiancé had suddenly gone missing. All it took was a couple of telephone calls to turn him up. Credit cards are such a blessing.

Seems the poor man had gotten cold feet and *adiosed* to Acapulco for a little R & R. After a brief chat with my quarry, during which I hinted at a possible law suit based on abandonment, he called my client, professed his undying love, and I got a nice, fat check. Sadly, it's been almost a month since I've been able to cover my costs.

I pocket my cell, crack open a second Diet Coke, and go over my last discussion with Arlene. Bottom line: Fin is up to no good. Why else would he hook my cousin on drugs? And the scariest part is, I don't know how far down the rabbit hole Arlene has gone with her lover.

And then, her comment about Fin promising her some meth from the batch they planned to cook tomorrow morning replays. And though Arlene didn't say as much, I have the definite impression that the cooking will take place at Fin's.

And there's the answer to my question. Where will I find Fin Holden? Presiding over his drug trade tomorrow morning. Bull's-eye.

At last, I have a good reason to call Chief Zandt. They don't believe Aunt Sallie was murdered? Fine. But they can't ignore a bona fide meth ring taking place under their very noses.

When I call Zandt, he's out. When I mention that I might have some information on the location of a local meth lab, the man tells me all drug busts are handled by Detective Liam Witcher, a narcotics investigator for Herkimer County, and gives me a number to call.

There's no answer, but a terse message asks for a name and a number and promises a return call within the next thirty minutes.

Fifteen minutes later my cell rings. I clear my throat a few times before I answer, "Alice Armington here."

"Then it really *is* you. I'll be damned."

"Pardon me?"

"Is this *the* Allie Armington? The one Fin Holden's dad cashiered out of Hotanawa?"

"Yes. Unfortunately, it is."

"This is Liam Witcher. Remember me? Fin used to call me Witch-man? I lived in that house on the highway that backed up to the Holdens' place."

The only "Witch-man" I remember was a clumsy, chunky kid with braces and an auburn mop.

"Of course I remember you," I lie.

"I heard about your aunt. I'm truly sorry to hear it. As I recall, she was a great lady."

"Yes she was," I say, trying to decide whether or not to address the fact that Witcher's colleagues have dropped a murder case at the behest of several powerful families. But, as far as I can tell, it's not Witcher's department that's been corrupted. So I decide to let it go. For now.

"Are you in charge of drugs?"

"Whoa, there. Better clarify what you mean by that?"

I laugh. "Guess that doesn't sound too good. They gave me your number when I mentioned I might have some information that you could use." I pause before I continue. "I heard a rumor about a meth lab operating in the area."

"Want to fill me in?"

I take a deep breath. "Would it be possible for you to come to Holden Cottage? I don't want to give you the information over my cell."

"I'm calling from Utica. I just got back from scuba diving in the Caymans with friends. But don't worry: I'm on my way."

CHAPTER 12

I've just finished a sandwich and a third Diet Coke when a tall, slender man sporting a killer-tan—definitely not a spring phenomenon in northern climes—steps onto the deck.

He moves forward while removing his dark blue bill cap to reveal a close-cut but well-shaped head. His sun-bleached auburn eyebrows and very long lashes accent hazel eyes flecked with gold and green.

His hand clutches mine in a powerful grip. "Liam Witcher."

"Of course, Detective Witcher, I remember you. It's just that I never expected you to be over six feet and so good-look ..."

My voice trails as a warning comes. *Watch it, Allie; he's probably married with a pack of kids.*

He gives me an infectious grin. "A stint in the Marines helped get rid of the lard, and I guess I was always going to be this tall. Runs in the family."

Then he looks me up and down. "I gotta say you turned out pretty much like us guys thought you would."

"Pardon?"

"We thought you were pretty cool back then. You showed a lot of spunk for a girl."

"Oh, thanks. Should I be flattered?"

Witcher gives me an indifferent shrug and changes the subject. "So, what have you been up to since your rather unceremonious departure?"

"Life in general, I guess. I graduated from high school, attended University of Texas, and UT Law. My first job was Assistant DA in Harris County."

"Looks like we sorta share parallel universes. I finished law at Columbia and kinda fell into what I'm doing now. Are you still in Houston?"

"Yes, but a couple of years ago I got tired of the crime scenes and left the DA for a Houston firm involved in real estate. Bad move. That market crashed and burned and my firm went with it. Now I'm solo—a lawyer and a licensed private investigator."

"You? A PI? Isn't that a step down?"

"Not really. Attorney-private investigator somehow seems to have a certain cachet in Texas and many times calls for a fatter paycheck."

"So, what are you investigating?"

"Nothing right now. As I mentioned on the phone, Arlene asked me to come up for a visit."

"How is ol' Butterball? I haven't seen her in years."

I feel a flush of resentment at my cousin's too-well-known nickname, but if truth be told, I might have used the same term until I saw her yesterday.

"Considering the circumstances, she's holding up pretty well. She left today for Wilmette with her older sister and her dad. They're flying Sallie's body back there for the funeral."

I wave toward a chair. "Have a seat. Want a beer or something?"

"Not right now, thanks." He waits until I'm settled, then says, "Okay. Let's hear it."

"I think you might be able to make a bust tomorrow morning."

"Who's your source?"

In order to protect Arlene, I decide to bend the truth a little. "I overheard a conversation. Thing is, I might be implicating an innocent person."

Detective Witcher goes into law mode. "Let me be the judge of that."

"It's supposed to go down at Holden's house."

Witcher's mouth drops for only a second, then he says, "You think Fin is involved in this?"

"It's his place, isn't it?"

He gives me a puzzled look, then murmurs, "This isn't new news. You say you overheard this info? Where?"

I lie. "In the Big M parking lot. Two men were standing next to a large truck and talking about the cook. But by the time I got to where they were, the truck was pulling away."

He locks his eyes to mine until I look away and murmur, "I've wasted your time. I'm sorry."

"Look, don't think I'm not grateful for your interest. It's just seems strange to me that someone at the Big M would be talking about cooking a batch of meth loud enough for you to hear."

My heartbeat ratchets up a notch, but I manage to look reassuring. "That's what I heard. Take it or leave it."

Witcher shrugs my words away and says, "I did a little checking and discovered that Fin rented the property to some corporation in New York City. Guess he didn't like being reminded of—"

I pick up on his inference. "Are you referring to the accident?" I ask as the usual wave of guilt ripples through me.

"Yeah. The way I hear it, even though the Holdens made the house wheelchair-friendly, Fin seldom came up to Fourth Lake after he got out of rehab.

"By then the Cornell campus was out of the question so he decided on NYU, leased a loft in SoHo, and after graduation he opted to stay in the city."

Witcher pauses, then says, "I know you must feel bad about what happened, but if truth be told, I think that accident was a relief."

My jaw drops. "Relief? How can being crippled for the rest of your life be a relief?"

"Mainly because Fin no longer had to live up to his dad's expecta-tions. Don't you remember how hard that old bastard made it for his firstborn son? You know Fin never was much for team sports."

"Yeah, he was really into tennis. Singles only, as I recall. No doubles for him. He had to be in control."

I nod in agreement. "You got that right. Fin always had to be the one in control. He was never a team player. You should know, you were part of it."

He ducks his head and gives me an embarrassed grin. "Hey there, your memory's a little too good."

"Yeah. And I remember how that expletive-deleted man demanded that Angela and I be sent home—me with my tail between my legs."

We both laugh at my poor joke, then I say, "But you still haven't told me why Fin was relieved?"

"His dad insisted Fin try out for the Cornell lacrosse team. The poor guy dreaded it. Fin knew way back then that he wasn't good enough—that he would never be an all-star."

Witcher shakes his head. "I'd be willing to bet that accident saved him a whole lot of grief."

"That's certainly a different perspective from mine."

"How so?"

"Well, I never considered that when I ran over Fin I was doing him a favor. Maybe he doesn't hate me so much after all."

Witcher laughs and rolls his eyes. "I don't think hate has ever been the operative word where you're concerned."

I feel my face heat as I remember that kiss. I can't help but wonder what might have happened if things hadn't gone the way they did. Then I stammer, "D-do you see Fin often?"

"Not since his Black Fly Reunion down in the Big Apple a couple of years ago. It's usually held in late April." He checks his watch, then shakes his head. "This is the second year I haven't gotten an invite. But then I've moved twice. Living in Old Forge got a little too tight for me so I moved to Utica. Takes an hour to get up here, but I spend the drive time organizing my days."

I want to tell Witcher that I know why there was no party this

April. Fin was up here playing daddy. Instead, I give him a hopeful smile. "I wouldn't worry too much. These days the post office isn't the most efficient forwarder."

"I sure hope it's only that. Fin doesn't exactly know what I do. And I don't have a clue what he does either. We've never taken time alone long enough to discuss our careers."

Witcher squints at the sky for a few seconds. When he turns back, he's all business. "We were tipped about Fin's place the day before I left for the Caymans. While I was away, my partner put a wire on an informant who made a buy last week."

"Then you have a warrant?"

Witcher nods and points to his jacket pocket. "Based on probable cause. But we have to catch them with the stuff. If we do, these people will serve some serious jail time. We were planning to make the bust tomorrow, and from what you've just told me, we should be right on schedule."

CHAPTER 13

After spending a sleepless night tossing and turning in my room at The Woods Inn, I shampoo and change into fresh clothing before heading back to the cottage.

I toast a couple of slices of whole grain and make a fresh pot of coffee before slipping on Alan Armington's warm fleece jacket. My Beretta 3032 Tomcat is in the right pocket, and my cell in the left.

It takes less than ten minutes to make my way along the highway to the Holden property and past the now-empty garage.

If I'm going to talk to Fin, then I've got to get there before Witcher and his team. We've got business to settle.

I pause to listen for any noise. Nothing. I take my Beretta off safety before I start down the side of the garage. I've barely started the trip when Witcher steps out, a Walther clutched in his right hand.

"What in hell are you doing here?"

We stare each other down as the seconds drag by, then I let out a sigh and lower my Beretta. I don't know Witcher well enough yet to tell him the real story so I come out with a weak, "I thought I might be able to help."

Witcher holsters his weapon. "Not necessary. I have backup stashed in the woods between here and the compound."

"But I won't get in the way. I promise."

"And I promise you won't." He points behind him toward the trees. "You'll have to exit this way—through these woods. Like now."

I give him a mute nod and turn to follow his order when tires screech down the gravel drive.

Witcher grabs my hand and yanks me along with him to stand behind the garage. Once there, he shoves me behind him, checks the magazine of his Walther, and waits.

One car door opens, followed by the sound of a second. "Got everything?"

The man's voice sounds like he's talking through a bunch of pebbles.

A woman answers. "Everything on the list, but you gotta hurry. I'm coming down fast. I need a bump and quick."

The screen door to the back porch creaks shut, then the door to the kitchen opens and closes.

Witcher lets out an exasperated sigh, then mutters, "There's no way you can leave now. We have to wait. It's pretty evident they're here to make that shit. We have to catch them with the product in their possession."

He points to the ground. "Guess we better have a seat. It's going to take a while to cook up the evidence."

After I manage to make it to a sitting position without making a klutzy fool of myself, he joins me, pulls out a couple of Snickers bars, and offers me one.

The rising sun warms us as we munch slowly on those wonderful chocolate, caramel, and nougat delights, while Witcher checks his watch every so often.

When the sun is above the trees, he stands, walks a few steps away, and makes a call on his cell. Once that's done, he returns to offer me a hand.

"The others are in place waiting for my signal. Look, this isn't going to be a walk in the park. These people could be armed and probably high by now. We know the fumes are toxic—not only to them but to us.

"The hazmat guys'll go in the front door. I'll cover the back—just in case." He checks his watch. "And that should be in about five minutes. By now that stuff should be perking along real nice."

"What do you want me to do?"

"Just stay here."

"But, I—"

At the sound of a second car pulling into the driveway, Witcher punches a number into his cell and after a few seconds says, "A car's just pulled in. I'm pretty sure it's just somebody making a buy. Not necessary to take the buyer at this juncture. Hold your positions until you hear from me."

A door slides open then the whir of a small motor rises to a sharp whine before it stops. Another small motor starts up and then we hear crunching across the limestone pebbles.

The back door opens and the man says. "Hey, dude, we didn't expect you today. What's up?"

Fin Holden's next words send a shiver down my spine. "Guess you heard what happened at the trailer park. Big explosion. Fire. It was crazy." There's a pause, then Fin says, "Sorry, Brenda. I'll try to find another place for you to hang your hat."

The man cuts in. "What happened?"

"Not sure. But the law is all over it. Bad news is, now that the trailer site has been destroyed, this'll really slow the operation down."

"Too bad. Just when things were about to crank up. What can I do ya for?"

"My fiancée's mother died and she's having a really rough time. I gave her all the ice I had, so that puts me flat out."

"You're in luck. Brenda and me has got a nice batch going. Don't we, babe?"

I look at Witcher. He's as shocked as I am.

After Fin's wheelchair whirs up the ramp and the back door snaps shut, Witcher mutters, "I never expected this."

He slides down to lean against the garage. "Fin's dad always flirted with the extra-legal, but I never thought Fin would break bad.

"When I first took this assignment I figured we were focusing on a couple of mom-'n'-pops. But with what I learned this morning, it seems we have bigger fish to fry."

"A bigger fish than Fin?"

"We know Fin's running a couple of labs. But if what he said is true about the explosion, then he's only got this site left. Word is there are some high-end types from out of the country moving in up here."

"Do you mean the Mafia?"

"Doubtful, most of their teeth have been pulled. Could be worse than them."

Witcher pulls out a card, scribbles a number on the back, and hands it to me. "You've got to get out of here. Now. Once you get to the highway, call my cell. That way, I'll know you're okay."

I start to protest, then realize Witcher is right. All I would do is hamper the operation. This is bigger than I thought it was. If I want to talk to Fin, I'm going to have to wait till he's behind bars.

I peer into the woods behind the garage. Not much cover there since the leaves are new. Still, I make a weak stab at staying. The PI in me wants to get in on the action. Besides, if Fin has anything to do with Aunt Sallie's death, I want to see him taken down.

"But I'm armed," I whisper. "And I know how to shoot."

"No way in hell. You're not one of us."

CHAPTER 14

I push my way through the tangles of underbrush until I'm a good fifteen yards into the woods. That's when I make the mistake of pausing to look behind me.

Through the leafy scrim I see Witcher, gun at the ready, flattened against the back of the garage.

The only part of the house I can see is a window on the second floor with the curtain pulled to one side. I freeze. Someone is at that window. Can they see me? Have they already seen me?

The breeze whispering through the branches is the only sound I hear except for the distant whoosh of traffic on the highway.

The minutes drag by as I stand still as a statue, staring back at the upstairs window. Then the curtain falls.

I punch Witcher's number in my cell and watch him raise his in response.

"Yeah?"

"I think I've been made."

"Then get to the highway. Now."

I don't need to hear another word. I jam my cell back in my pocket and plunge through the dense undergrowth, stumbling crazily whenever my foot catches on a root. Each time I fall, I land on my left knee, and after the third or fourth time, a sharp pain accompanies each step I take.

The highway is only a few yards ahead when I hear the shots. I stop and turn to peer through the long expanse of trees but can see nothing through the leafy green curtain.

I ignore the nagging pain in my knee and, with the Beretta clutched in my right hand, turn to retrace my steps.

By the time I make the garage several minutes have passed. Witcher is down, on his side, facing away from me. But the blossoming bloodstain on the upper back of his shirt tells the tale.

I pocket my weapon and kneel. "Witcher?"

No response. I check his carotid and feel a steady pulse and my adrenaline surges in relief.

When I hear footsteps crunching on the limestone, I stand, pull my weapon, and get ready to shoot.

Stupid me. I didn't even consider that someone else might have seen me return. But at least I'll get a couple of shots in before they get me.

Really stupid me. I'm aimed in the wrong direction.

From behind comes the command, "Drop your weapon. Hands in the air."

I do as the man says and then a second man in a hazmat suit, gun at the ready, steps into view.

He stares at me a minute, then raises the protective cover from his face. "Cool it, Evans. This is the woman Witcher told us about. Armington? Right?"

I let out my held breath. "Right. What happened?"

"We heard shots, then a car and a van tore out of here before we could make it across the clearing.

"We entered the house to run a brief reconnaissance, and it looks like they were somehow able to take the evidence with them—even though you can still smell the meth. Looks like they were done cooking when something spooked them."

"I'm afraid that might have been me. Detective Witcher sent me through the woods to the highway. I was about fifteen yards into the woods when I turned to look back. That's when I saw one of the upstairs curtains pulled to one side. I'm pretty sure someone must have seen me and come looking."

"So you think that's who shot Detective Witcher?"

"To the best of my knowledge, there were at least two men and a woman in the house. One of the men was in a wheelchair, so I'm pretty sure he couldn't have gotten back here. That leaves the other man or maybe the woman, but—"

Witcher's raspy groan interrupts me. "Hey, don't just stand there yakking, get me something to plug this wound."

After the men disappear around the corner, Witcher says, "Is there blood on my back and a hole in my shirt?"

"Yes."

"That's good news. It's the exit wound. Thank God I won't have someone digging around in my shoulder all night."

He struggles to sit, then collapses back to the ground. "Owww. Not a great move. Am I bleeding?'

I kneel beside him. "I don't see any new blood, but that doesn't mean a thing. I'm a sorry nurse."

He lets out a breath. "I'm an even sorrier patient, but they're going to haul me to Utica. It's SOP.

"I'll have one of the guys run you back to the cottage. Ordinarily, I'd have him stay until I came back, but I've got two men out sick and we're down to a skeleton crew."

"Actually, I have a room at The Woods Inn. I can lay low there until I hear from you."

"No!" He shakes his head. "Not a good move. That's the first place they look. I know it sounds safer to be in a public situation, but if they somehow get to you, all they have to do is stick a gun in your side and escort you out the front door of the hotel. Once that happens, we'll have no clue where to find you."

I retrace his logic. Strange as it seems, it makes sense. Sort of. I check the bottom of my stomach. No stones, not even a pebble. Witcher must have had some experience with this type of situation before.

"No problem. I'm an armed PI, nobody messes with me."

He seems to buy into my bravado. "And I believe it." He checks his watch. "It's just past ten. I'll come get you after I get this hole in my shoulder fixed. Any place you can move your car so it can't be seen?"

"I suppose I could park it in one of the garages that are on the drive just below the cottage."

"Then do that first thing. Let's face it: If they saw you, they're going to come after you. The good news is *they* don't want to be seen either, so you'll be safe at the cottage until dark. But don't worry, I'll be back long before dark to move you to a safe haven."

I don't know whether to be appreciative of Witcher's concern, or affronted that he doesn't seem to think I can take care of myself.

"I'm a big girl, you know," I say, a little annoyed.

"I know you are," he says, mustering a grin. "But the big girls are the easiest to find."

CHAPTER 15

The afternoon is pretty much gone by the time I grab a bite to eat and check out of Woods. In the parking lot, I place my roller-bag in the trunk of the rental, drive to Hotanawa, and stash the car facing out in one of the lower garages.

I feel a little nauseous, nervous that I've now become a target. If Fin and his druggies are responsible for Aunt Sallie's death, then I have no doubt they'll do anything to shut me up. Even murder.

Once in the cottage, I check the fireplace to be sure there are no embers from the night before and turn off the oven.

The right pocket of my fleece jacket bulges with my Beretta and the left holds my cell that I have on vibrate so the ring won't attract attention.

I glance at my watch. It's past six and the sun is low in the sky, but still no call from Witcher.

When I pull out my cell, my stomach flips. The battery is just short of gone, and the charger is stashed in my roller-bag. How could I be so stupid? Then I smile to myself, when I realize I have another out.

Gun at the ready, I sidle into the back hall and lift the receiver of the wall phone.

Nothing. The land line is dead.

Mind reeling, I hang up as my heart rips to double time, and I crumple onto the back stairs.

Think. Think. Take a few deep breaths and make a plan. It's obvious someone has been watching the cottage.

I try a few more inhales, take stock of my situation, and then realize that I'm only a few feet from the safest place in the cottage.

I ease up the stairs to the darkened landing. When I was a kid that was the one place I could easily elude whoever was after me. Only back then it was Olly Olly Ox. Right now it's pure desperation.

The good news is that from this perch I can see into the kitchen as well as into the living room, and unless someone knows about my "safe place," no one can see me.

When they come, and they will, I'll at least have a chance.

The minutes drag by as the light fades. It's nearing seven. Witcher said he would be back. But now I'm not so sure. Maybe his wound was more serious than he thought. Maybe... No! I can't go there. Witcher was very much alive the last time I saw him.

A half hour passes before I hear footsteps descending the steep stone steps. For only a second, I feel relief. Then, when I realize there are at least two people descending the steps—maybe three—I shrink back and ready my weapon. With luck I can take out two, but bagging the third will be almost impossible.

The sliding door opens and, after a few shuffles, the light in the kitchen floods the room.

I jerk back in response, then lean forward until the kitchen floor comes into view.

At first all I see is a pair of running shoes, then the square brass belt buckle composed of Hotanawa's four Indian arrowheads with each tip meeting the others in the middle.

I remember that design so well. The buckles were highly prized— worn only by males who won the compound's sports contests on the Fourth and on Labor Day. Girls were awarded barrettes or bracelets.

My thoughts are jammed to the present to see Fin standing in the kitchen doorway just below my perch.

It's all I can do to muffle my gasp. Fin is not crippled—not at all.

I lower my weapon to the stair tread and pull out my iPhone. I wait until Fin reaches for the wall phone, then press the camera button. Nothing happens. Not enough juice left to take a picture.

Fin lifts the receiver, then slams it down. "Dead."

When the second man moves to the doorway he says, "She must have cut the line before she beat it out of here earlier this afternoon."

Fin shoves past him back into the kitchen. The oven door opens. "Barely warm. She's been gone for some time."

"What now? She knows all about the meth. She was with them."

The oven door clicks shut. "Taking care of Allie won't be a problem. Her next stop will be Chicago for her aunt's funeral and I'll be right there with her."

"Okay, okay, but what about the narcs?"

"Now that Witcher is down, those guys will be out of the picture for a while."

"I sure hope that's true. His involvement is a major pain in the ass."

Fin moves from the kitchen into the living room and pulls open a few drawers. "I know it's here. Arlene said it was. You sure you went through everything?"

"Everything in the living room. Isn't that where she said it would be?"

"Yeah." There's a long pause before Fin speaks again. "You're sure it went down just like you said?"

"Why would I lie? We wore the masks, rushed into her bedroom. Then we gave her the hypo and searched the house. But I'm telling you the truth, we never once saw the mother."

Fin's voice drops. "Any way you cut it, that woman was murdered and right now you two are the only suspects."

"As far as I'm concerned that's moot. The narcs don't know who we are." There's a brief silence before he asks, "Or do they?"

"I can't see how. Since you both were wearing masks and gloves, Arlene can't identify you. And, even though I'm not exactly sure what Allie knows, I can handle her."

There's a long pause before the other man responds. "Hey, just so we have this straight. You made the plan. You sent us." He pauses, then says, "Where in hell do you think that tiara could be?"

I slowly slide back to lean against the wall, my mind scattered in a hundred directions by this new information. If what the other man says is true, then Fin, even though he's a druggie, and possibly a thief, is not a murderer.

But what about the tiara? Did poor Aunt Sallie sacrifice her life for the fake diamond tiara Arlene and I used to fight over when we were little?

I think back to those wonderful rainy days when Aunt Sallie would get an old boathook stored in the second floor linen closet and pull down the stairs to the attic.

Arlene and I would slowly climb up the stairs, and then wait for Aunt Sallie to join us, and turn on the light. Once she was sure we were okay, she would leave us to spend the next few hours playing dress up with the old clothes stored in a large musty trunk.

There were wonderful sparkly high heels, pink and white feather boas, and several strings of long fake pearls. And of course the prized "diamond" tiara. But since there was only *one* tiara, we had to flip a coin to see who would wear it first.

Why did Arlene tell Fin the tiara was real? To impress him? That is so *not* the Arlene I knew, but then, she was always desperate for his love and meth addiction changes people.

And now there's a brand new twist: If the other guy with Fin was telling the truth, then who killed Aunt Sallie?

I can't think about that now. Witcher must be so badly injured that they've stashed him in some hospital in Utica and I'm stuck here on the landing. And with Fin and his accomplice below me, I can't afford to make one false move.

When I take a deep breath, willing the air to flow silently into my lungs, the footsteps stop.

The second man says, "Did you hear something?"

A minute passes. A minute that seems like an eternity.

"You're just spooked," Fin says finally. "Come on. We're not going to find it tonight."

The men leave the kitchen as I breathe a sigh of relief. But there's no way I'm coming down from my hiding place now, not when they might still be lurking nearby.

There's only one thing to do.

Wait.

CHAPTER 16

"Miss Armington? Detective Witcher sent me."

The policeman's voice urged me from my fitful sleep on the landing and I rose from my secret place to follow him down the stairs to the back hall.

It was well past midnight when the uniform, flashlight in one hand and his weapon at the ready, led me to the lower garage where I opened the trunk and retrieved the cell charger.

The patrol car trailed me down the highway to the Fastrac in Old Forge, where I gassed up, grabbed a grande-sized styro of coffee, and got something to munch on while I drove on to Syracuse.

There's a lot of new information to integrate with what I gleaned from Arlene. As I make the drive, I start to fill in the gaps. From the conversation I overheard, it sounds like Fin and his goonies aren't responsible for the murder. They may have gotten my cousin hooked on meth, but they didn't murder Aunt Sallie.

So who did?

One thing's for sure: Fin knows more than he's saying. And if Sallie's death had something to do with the tiara, then maybe Fin is the one who can give me a clue.

When I check my rejuvenated cell, there are four messages: the first from Detective Witcher, profusely apologizing for sending someone else in his place. It seems his wound ultimately required surgery to close it properly and he was to be hospitalized overnight.

The second is from my Uncle Aiden, who broke the connection and then called back minutes later saying that the funeral would take place in three days. He named the church and the time and hung up. His pain was more than evident in his pinched voice and the shuddering sighs between his words as if naming the date and the time of the funeral meant that his beloved Sallie was really gone.

The last message is from my dad. "Your mother and I are flying in tomorrow afternoon. Staying at the Northbrook Hilton. Unless I hear otherwise, I'm getting you a room there too."

It's past two when I crash at the Marriott Courtyard near Hancock Airport. I sleep like the dead until my ten a.m. wake-up call pulls me into the day.

∽✕∾

After snagging the next American Airlines flight to O'Hare and taking a taxi to the Northbrook Hilton, I check in and go to my parent's room.

The ready welcome in my father's eyes and his warm bear hug is enough to sustain me through my mother's usual disapproving once-over and her "Can't you do something with that hair?" as she carefully embraces me with her lobster claws.

Dad fills me in on what's happening as we drive to the other Armingtons' home. Once Ardythe told her father about her sister's condition, plans were made, and when Arlene arrived home, the family doctor and her new guardian were waiting.

Since then she has been sedated and confined to her room. After the funeral service and the reception at their home, Arlene will enter a rehab facility.

I shove the latest developments at Holden Cottage to one side of my mind and spend the next day helping the other Armingtons.

My main job is to receive the endless casseroles supplied by a stream of concerned widows whose faces fall when they discover Uncle Aiden is not in the kitchen.

And finally, there I stand, third in the second pew, which accommodates only six.

On our side of the aisle the other Armingtons command the front pew. Aiden is on the aisle. Next to him is a visibly shaken Alan, who arrived from Hong Kong only yesterday, leaving his family behind. Ardythe and her husband Doug are next to him. Their two sons, Geoff and Sam, have been relegated to our row so that Arlene and her keeper, a very tall, muscular woman, can fit in.

Uncle Aiden slumps forward, the wind blown from his sails by his beloved's sudden and horrific death.

Alan stands erect, though his face is pale. His left fist keeps clenching again and again. His right arm comforts his father's back.

I can't see Ardythe, though occasionally, when her shoulders shake, Doug pulls her to him in sympathy.

Arlene's face is expressionless—numbed by sedatives, I suppose. Though she's been thoughtfully put together, her clothes are two sizes too large and hang on her like drying sheets on a clothesline.

I haven't asked Ardythe or Alan about their sister. Now is not the time. Now is the time to say goodbye.

The church is jammed. Standing room only. Later I hear that the church's side yards were filled as well.

Everybody loved Sallie. I look at the cross on the altar and murmur, "I promise I won't rest until I find who did this."

When my father bends his head my way with question in his eyes, I smile and shake my head. No need for the Armington clan to know the gruesome facts surrounding Aunt Sallie's death until I can produce the bastard who murdered her.

Preceded by the pallbearers, including the elder Walton and Taylor, and young Tommy Napier (I can't look at him without wanting to wring the neck of his snide sister), Sallie's flower-laden casket rolls toward the altar to the strains of "Onward Christian Soldiers."

As I look at the representatives the families have sent, I can barely suppress my rage that these people want everyone to think Sallie killed herself, all to protect their little enclave of vacation homes. How petty and self-centered. How wrong.

"Onward Christian Soldiers" was Sallie's favorite hymn. She used to belt it out at the top of her lungs on the Armington's annual climb up Bald Mountain to enjoy the spectacular view down the Fulton Chain of Lakes.

I glance toward the aisle as the pallbearers pass and freeze. There, next to the line of honorary pallbearers who are already seated in a row of metal chairs, is Fin Holden, his body slumped in a motor-driven wheelchair.

What a fraud. What else is he lying about?

He must feel my stare because he turns slowly my way to give me a solemn nod.

If he thinks he's going to get off that easy, he's got another thing coming.

I try to concentrate on the rest of the service. The time to confront Fin will come very soon.

CHAPTER 17

The Armingtons' rambling two-story house sits on a bluff over-looking Lake Michigan. Though hardly a mansion, it is comfortable and welcoming.

I remember Aunt Sallie saying that she fell in love with this house the minute she saw it one day in May before the family made its annual pilgrimage to Fourth Lake. She had been visiting a college friend from Northwestern who lived a little north of Wilmette.

When she and Aiden married, the house she had rhapsodized over during many of her family's meals was a surprise gift from her parents. Signed, sealed, and delivered when the newlyweds returned from a honeymoon in Hawaii.

I'm just about to make my way to the long porch across the back of the house when Tommy Napier steps forward to give me a big hug. I stiffen.

"Allie," he says. "Sad time. We were all so grieved to hear of Sallie's passing."

Not grieved enough to think twice about killing the case.

"Yes, Sallie's *murder* took us all by surprise," I say, making sure to put emphasis where it's due.

Tommy's eyes widen at the word "murder" but his next words are overridden by the low whine of a wheelchair motor.

The crowd parts as Fin Holden rolls forward to stop beside us.

He smiles. "Hello, Tommy. I didn't expect to see you in the lineup."

Tommy reddens. "I'm here for Alan. But I can't quite figure out why Mr. Armington asked you to be one of Sallie's pallbearers."

Fin gives him a surprised look. "Oh? Haven't you heard? Arlene and I are engaged to be married."

Shock stuffs Tommy's face. "You've got to be kidding."

"Not kidding at all." Fin moves his wheelchair to nudge Tommy out of our conversation. "Would you excuse us?"

Tommy makes a hasty retreat. I turn to Fin. "That was rude."

He ignores my jibe. "Well, well, well, if it isn't Little Allie-Oopsie."

I glare down at him, my face flushed with anger and embarrassment at his use of what I once treasured as his pet name for me.

"I'm surprised to see you, Fin. I hear you've been quite busy at Holden Cottage."

I detect a slight flush in Fin's cheeks, but he shrugs it off and plasters on a grin. "I have no idea what you mean by that, but when your uncle asked me to be a pallbearer, I couldn't refuse. Cousin Sallie would have been my mother-in-law if she hadn't had such an unfortunate accident." He pauses to let his take on Sallie's death sink in and then smiles. "I was deeply touched by his inclusion."

He reaches for my hand and presses. "I'm so sorry about your family's loss. Please accept my condolences."

When I finally manage to yank my hand from his grip, he shakes his head. "I thought you'd be glad to see me. Aren't you going to congratulate me?"

"Congratulate you? What for? Hooking Arlene on meth? But that's old copy now. Frankly, I'm more interested in the latest news about your baby."

That gets his attention. "Arlene told you?"

"She tells me everything. In case you've forgotten, we're like sisters."

Fin slowly shakes his head. "Don't believe everything she says."

"Then there is no child?"

"Did I say that?"

"Not exactly."

He pauses, then says, "Once Arlene is clean and sober, we'll share a real family."

"Over my dead body!"

Fin gives me a cold smile. "Be careful what you wish for, Allie. Sometimes wishes come true."

CHAPTER 18

It's late when Dad, Mother, and I say our goodbyes to the other Armingtons. Arlene and her father have long since retired, as has Alan, who is making the long flight back to Hong Kong first thing tomorrow.

After we return to the hotel, and even though it's been a long, sad day, I announce, "I'm too pumped to go down just yet. Think I'll hit the bar."

To my surprise, Dad offers to join me, saying he has something he wants to discuss with me before leaving Chicago.

Mother's eyebrows arch. "Should I come, too?"

He gives her a dismissive hug. "Oh, darling, this legal stuff will bore you to tears. And you look exhausted. Why don't you go on up and get comfortable? I won't be long."

She gives him one of her "if looks could kill" glances, and before I can offer my arms, she turns and marches toward the elevator bank.

Once we've settled in a booth and ordered our drinks, Dad pulls a long, fat envelope from his inside pocket. "Aiden gave me this just before he retired this evening. It's for you."

I take it and see that it's addressed to me. The return address reads: Hatcher, Wilsey, Timmons, LLP, Chicago, Illinois.

"What's this?"

"What's in the envelope is going to surprise you—at least it did me."

I shiver as I slowly open the back flap and remove an official-looking document. The cover letter informs me that Aunt Sallie's last will dated in early May has included me as an heir.

I look up to see Dad's eyebrows raised in anticipation.

"What on earth would Aunt Sallie leave me?"

"Just read," he says.

I wade through the boilerplate until I see my name halfway down the second page and gasp. Aunt Sallie has left Holden Cottage to me along with a sizeable amount of annual income from a trust she created for upkeep of the place.

"Oh, my God. How can this be ...?"

My heart races as I read, then re-read the words; my emotions torn between my grief for Aunt Sallie and the shock of such an unexpected gift.

It's then I remember Arlene's surprisingly sarcastic retorts before the family left for Chicago. Of course she must have already known. Arlene has wanted Holden Cottage since she was old enough to know about wanting. I gasp as the unbidden accusation rises once again. Oh, Arlene. No!

I shove that thought away and murmur, "I can't believe this."

"Well, my dear, believe it." Dad's next words are a welcome balm for my concerns. "Aiden, despite his grief, told me he's very pleased for you. Personally, I think it's because he won't have to return to the scene of the crime, which he most likely would have had to do if Arlene had inherited."

Then after a long pause, my father says, "Of course, you must realize that Arlene will not be at all happy about this. But, I don't think you'll have to face her quite yet. Poor girl has a much bigger problem to deal with."

I want to tell my dad what I suspect: that Arlene already knew of the changes that her mother had made in May. But not before I find some concrete evidence.

"What should I do? I don't want Arlene to think I—she's wanted Holden forever."

He lets out a long breath, then says, "All I can say is that Sallie, knowing how deeply Arlene felt about Holden, must have had a very good reason to leave the cottage to you. My advice is to not make any decision until you get all the facts."

⊙⊱⊰⊙

When my parents stage an early exit the next morning, I don't make an effort to say goodbye. No point in hashing over the latest development about Holden Cottage with Mother. She wouldn't understand.

A night of restless sleep hasn't solved my dilemma. I'm still torn about what I should do next. And Fin's parting words didn't do much to assuage my fears that he might have developed a murderous streak.

I'm halfway through breakfast when my cell rings and Liam Witcher starts in before I can say hello. "Don't you ever answer your messages? I've been waiting two days to hear from you."

"Sorry, funerals take precedence over returning phone calls. How are you?"

"Sore as hell, but the prognosis is excellent. How did the funeral go?"

"As well as can be expected. The other families were there, all oozing with sympathy over Aunt Sallie's 'suicide.' I know you didn't know my aunt, but I guarantee you, there is something fishy going on. And it smells like obstruction of justice."

Witcher is silent. When he speaks, his voice is a little gruff. "It's really not my department, Allie."

We're silent for another long moment. "Well then. I guess I should keep my comments to drugs and narcotics, huh?" I say, trying to keep the edge out of my voice.

I tell him about Fin's visit to the cottage and that he was walking just fine. And after repeating the conversation between Fin and his accomplice, I say, "The other man admitted to drugging Arlene, but told Fin he and his buddy never saw Aunt Sallie."

"You actually heard him say that?"

"Yes. Seems he and his accomplice were looking for a tiara. But the only tiara I know about is the one Arlene and I used when we played dress-up and I can assure you, it was a fake."

A long silence follows before Witcher says, "Unfortunately, after our bust went bad, the suspects have dropped below the radar."

I suppress the surge of guilt flowing through me. The bust didn't go down because of me. I had blown everything.

At that, I make a small effort to make things right. "Well, Fin is here in Wilmette. At least he was yesterday. All slumped over in his motorized wheelchair, playing the crippled, bereaved fiancé to the hilt. My Uncle Aiden even asked him to be an honorary pallbearer."

Witcher is silent for a few seconds. "We don't have a thing to hang on him now except suspicion, and he's out of my jurisdiction."

"Well, you can blame me for that. I was the one who blew the bust."

"Hey, don't beat up on yourself too much. I've blown a few myself. Comes with the job. Mind if I ask what do you plan to do next?"

It's then I tell him about Aunt Sallie's gift.

"No way!" There's a long pause and then he says, "But I thought Arlene—"

"So did I. Frankly, I don't exactly know what to do next. Aunt Sallie meant the world to me when I was growing up. I'm honored she thought of me in this way. But, I'm not too eager to move into the scene of the crime. It's just too creepy."

"Yeah, I guess that would be true for me as well. Of course, the case has been ruled a suicide, no crime committed. Sorry—I know that's not what you want to hear."

My heartbeat steps up a notch as scattered thoughts form in my mind. I'm angry at Witcher, but what did I expect? He works with them.

But then another thought dawns on me. The police have all but closed the case; they're focusing their energy and manpower on the drug bust. That means that, if I went back to Inlet, I could investigate

Aunt Sallie's murder my way, on my time ... without any interference from the authorities.

For a second, I wonder if I've lost my mind. Am I really going to go back alone and track down a killer?

Of course I am. I'm a PI and a lawyer. If the police have been coerced and corrupted, who is going to bring Sallie's killer to justice? I am!

CHAPTER 19

Before I go back to Hotanawa, I want to try and straighten out the mess between Arlene and me. But there could be a major problem with that. If the plans are still on go, Arlene is being hospitalized for detox today.

When I call Duncan, tell him my problem, and ask for some extended vacation time, he reminds me that I don't require his permission since I'm an independent agent.

Then he adds, "But if you want my opinion, I think you need to sort out the details with your cousin as soon as possible. Matters like this have a way of escalating."

My enthusiasm is further blunted when I call Uncle Aiden to tell him my thoughts.

"I wish that were possible, Allie, but ..." He let's out a sad sigh. "As you know, Sis is entering the hospital today to begin her detox. Thank God for Myra Stetson. Having that woman on board has saved us all."

The woman in the first pew with Arlene was tall and muscular—almost masculine. Still, there was a softness about her eyes and ready smile.

Aiden's low voice interrupts. "And, you might as well hear the bad news. I felt I had to tell Sis about Holden Cottage before she was hospitalized.

"It comes as no surprise that she is very hurt and angry. She said she's sure you must have used undue influence and intends to bring a suit against you when she's well."

"But Uncle Aiden, you know that I would never—"

"Of course. You're like a sister to her and I'm sure when she's drug free, you girls will be able to work something out."

I try to brush aside Arlene's sarcasm before she left the cottage because we have been thick as thieves for as long as I can remember. But now she's threatening to sue me. I've never known her to be so angry or vindictive. But then, I've never known her to be addicted to meth.

Suddenly, that first inkling I felt about Arlene comes through loud and clear. Maybe she could be capable of murder. What if, in her drug-addled brain, she was so desperate to inherit the cottage that, the night she and Sallie fought, Arlene, high on meth, didn't know what she was doing?

It sounds crazy, but the possibility of Arlene turning violent nags at me. I need to see her as soon as possible. I've got questions, and I need answers.

"Is there any chance I could see her before she goes in?" I ask Uncle Aiden.

"I'll ask, but don't count on it."

Aiden covers the mouthpiece with his hand. The conversation is muted but with each passing sentence, my hopes raise a little.

Finally, Aiden says. "Sis has agreed to see you. Myra thinks it might help. How quickly can you get here?"

"Within the hour. Thank you so much."

"Don't thank me. Thank Myra."

I throw my clothes in the roller-bag, then call American to book the flight to Syracuse. I take the last seat available on one leaving at 3:25.

Witcher answers his cell, and I say, "I'm landing in Syracuse on American at six. Can we meet?"

⌗

When Myra Stetson opens the door, I pull my roller-bag to one corner of the entry and extend my hand. "Thank you for this."

She gives me a cautionary look. "Don't expect too much, if anything at all."

I follow her to the sun porch to see a welcoming smile on my uncle's face—a sharp contrast to the sullen pout on my cousin's.

I make my first mistake when I lean down to hug Arlene. She pushes me away. "Don't touch me, you traitor."

Uncle Aiden, pretending not to notice his daughter's hostility, gives me a welcoming hug and offers me a glass of lemonade as he says, "We've made Sallie's concoction to substitute for my usual midmorning coffee break. Myra says too much coffee isn't good."

I take the glass and settle in the nearest seat as my uncle returns to his favorite wicker chair.

Tears push at the back of my eyes as I remember sharing lemonades with Aunt Sallie during those wonderful hot afternoons on the deck at Fourth Lake. But the horrific moment when I looked down to discover her crumpled body flashes before me.

And what if I'm looking at the woman who had something to do with it?

Whatever really went down that morning, I feel sure that Arlene knows more about what happened to her mother than she is telling.

The tension between Arlene and me is so palpable that I can hardly breathe, but I manage a sip or two while I gather my wits. "Arlene, thank you so much for agreeing to meet with me. I'm very anxious to try and make the new ownership of Holden Cottage as manageable for the two of us as possible."

Arlene gives a derisive snort. "That cottage is mine, not yours. I'll be bringing a suit against you as soon as I'm out."

She slams down her half-empty glass on the wicker table and leaves the porch with Myra Stetson in hot pursuit.

My uncle slowly shakes his head. "Please try to understand, half of it is the drugs, the other—"

Footsteps sound and Myra reappears. "I'm sorry that didn't go so well, but once Arlene is drug-free and on the program, things will be much better."

I give them both an enthusiastic nod, even though my heart is breaking. "Of course, of course. All I want is to work something out with Arlene."

I'm surprised to hear my next words. "I've decided to go back to Syracuse as soon as I can get a flight.

"The police aren't looking for Sallie's killer because they've closed the murder investigation. I can't . . . I won't let that happen."

Aiden stands. "Are you sure that's the wisest course of action, Allie? There might be people who won't want you around."

"Well then, too bad for them."

There's an awkward silence before Aiden says, "I haven't been out since Sallie . . ." He pauses to tie a weak smile on his lips and then says, "But it's time I started getting about. I'd like to take you to the airport. What time is your flight?"

"I should be there around two, two-fifteen."

"Then we could have a bite before?"

Myra gives the two of us a wide grin. "Oh, how wonderful! A nice outing would do you so much good, Mr. Armington. While the two of you are having lunch, I'll get Arlene ready, and when you get back we can both help her check in."

CHAPTER 20

Uncle Aiden has chosen a restaurant in Mount Prospect, a few miles north of O'Hare. Despite the fact that it's in a strip mall and sports vinyl tablecloths, the lunch menu is so yummy it takes me a good five minutes to finally decide on the baby spinach salad with warm beets followed by wonton raviolis filled with rock shrimp.

My uncle chooses the grilled vegetable Swiss tartine and orders a nice bottle of Sancerre to accompany our choices.

He waits until the wine is served before he brings up his daughter, his voice filled with pain. "I want to believe that Sis will stay clean after she goes through the detox and the program at Hazelden, but in my heart I feel she can't wait to slide out of our clutches.

"Of course Ms. Stetson will be a major factor in Sis's recovery. Apparently, the woman has a sterling reputation with lots of successes under her belt. Thank the Lord she just came off a case and was available."

He's offering me the perfect opportunity to tell him everything I know. It would be best to wait until we're back in the car, but he needs time to digest what I'm about to say.

"Uncle Aiden?" I reach across the table to cover his hand with mine, and then spill the horrible truth.

"How much do you know about Arlene and Fin?"

He shrugs and says, "Apparently, Fin made contact with Arlene just after we returned from our Thanksgiving trip to Houston. After a few dates he proposed and then asked her to move with him to Inlet."

"Well, the timing is a little off. Actually, by several months. Arlene told me they secretly started going out last summer."

Aiden's eyebrows shoot up in surprise. "Is that so?"

When I nod, he says, "In the past few years Sis seldom visited Sallie and me except for the holidays and, of course, up at the lake. We knew how she treasured her visits, but then her business took precedent and her trips grew more infrequent, lasting only a few days."

I think back to my sad time during the past Thanksgiving and how having Arlene at my side had been such a blessing. She had to have been almost five months pregnant then. But first pregnancies are late to show and Arlene had always been a butterball. Now, after only a few months, the tables have turned.

"Christmas Day was the last time I saw Sis until ..."

His shoulders slump at the inference of Sallie's murder. "But Allie, Arlene is an adult. And we both respected her privacy. To tell you the truth, I didn't even know she had left the Board of Trade."

He lets out a long sigh. "And though Sis is well into adulthood, she's made some very poor choices, especially Fin. She knew I never cared for the father or his son."

I take a sip of the flinty wine and say, "I hate to be the bearer of bad news, but I have it from a good source that Fin has been running a couple of meth labs near Inlet—one in his family home right next door to Hotanawa."

I briefly describe the events that happened the day they departed for Wilmette and how Liam Witcher had been shot.

"But the kicker was, even though Fin knew the Feds were onto them, he and another man returned to Holden Cottage after you and the girls left.

"I was hiding on the back stairs landing and heard them talking. They were looking for the diamond tiara that Arlene and I used to play dress-up with. For some reason Arlene told Fin the tiara was real."

My uncle rears back. "Slow down, slow down. Are you saying my Sallie was murdered because of that damned tiara?"

"That's what Fin and this man seemed to be looking for."

I decide not to add to his grief by telling what the second man said about not seeing Sallie. Or that Arlene and Sallie had argued about Fin and the cottage and that Arlene could be the prime suspect. It's too awful that I'm even thinking it. And it's not what Uncle Aiden needs to hear right now.

Instead I throw out another thought. "Could it be that Aunt Sallie caught onto what Fin was up to? If she re-wrote her will in May ...?"

He nods. "The lawyer told her she only had to add a codicil but she wanted a completely new will written."

I suddenly remember the hastily scrawled addition to the Big M shopping list. What if Sallie was trying to deliver a message in her final moments? What if she was trying to let us know what she'd found out?

The final word on the list looked like "Fish." But what if it was "Fin"?

"Were there other changes?" I ask, hardly able to suppress my excitement over this new clue.

"Yes. Sallie had Sis's part of the inheritance pretty much tied up. I told her such a move was useless because Sis had already made plenty of money on her own."

He smiles, eyes filling with pride. "That girl has an almost psychic knack for picking just the right stocks."

It suddenly occurs to me that Arlene, smart as she is financially, might not be as well protected as she could be. "Do you have Arlene's power of attorney?"

"Power of attorney?" He shakes his head. "I never even considered—is it necessary?"

"Absolutely. At least while she's undergoing detox and the program at Hazelden. Do you know if anyone else has access to her bank accounts?"

The light dawns and Aiden says, "You think Fin could be after her money?"

"Maybe, maybe not. A successful meth operation generates plenty of cash. But it's plain to me Arlene has been, and probably still is, very much under Fin's control."

"Maybe I should consult a local attorney."

"I don't think you need to go that far. I'm pretty sure you can download an Illinois version of a POA from the Internet. The only problem will be getting Arlene to sign it in front of a notary and witnesses."

The spinach salad with warm beets arrives and I turn my attentions to that for a few minutes before saying, "I sincerely hope Arlene and I can work something out about Holden Cottage. I know how much she wants it."

What I don't say is: Just how much does she want it? And what lengths would she go to get it ... especially if Fin Holden were involved?

CHAPTER 21

My heart flutters against my chest when Witcher pulls me to him in an unexpected hug.

His voice is gruff. "Gosh, it's good to see you. I didn't exactly plan on missing you this much."

I step away, my face flushed with heat. I want to believe that he's a good guy, but he's with the police. These guys are eating out of the Napiers' hands—and the other self-absorbed families who care more about reputation than justice. I can't trust him. I'll work with him to get the information I need to solve the case, but the absolute last thing I want is to get close to him.

So then, why does it feel so good when he says he missed me?

"How's your shoulder?" I say, trying to maintain as professional a demeanor as possible.

He moves it and grimaces. "Okay, I guess. Hurts when the weather changes." He checks me over. "Hope you've got a heavier jacket. Supposed to rain and drop to forty tonight. Talk about global warming! At this rate we may never see summer."

Witcher pulls out of the airport and heads south on towards the city on I-81.

"Hungry?"

I nod. "Two packages of pretzels and a Diet Coke didn't do too much for me."

"Perfect! Got just the place. Quiet, good drinks, passable food."

I'm starving, but dinner with Witcher feels a little like eating with the enemy. "Don't worry about it if you're in a time crunch. I have to retrieve my rental from Hertz."

He grins. "I've got all the time in the world."

Well, so much for that.

In minutes we're settled across from each other in the back booth of a cozy bar with drinks in hand and our orders taken. We pretty much have the place to ourselves except for a few stragglers on the stools up front.

"So, Fin is still in the Chicago area?"

"No clue. But I can assure you he's still hoping to find the tiara."

Witcher snorts. "You said it was paste."

"That's what we were told."

"You saying it could be real?"

I think about it for a few seconds. The possibility that the diamonds were real hadn't occurred to me before. "We played with it all the time when we were kids. Don't you think that if it were real it would have been stashed in a vault?"

"Maybe your aunt didn't know it was the real McCoy. Because if it is, we could be talking mega-bucks."

Witcher's sudden interest in the tiara strikes me as a little strange. What if ... but no, that's impossible! He was shot, for goodness sake. Surely he couldn't have anything to do with ...

I change the subject. "So, what about the meth?"

"We have a 24/7 on Fin's house and what's left of the trailer. So far no movement in either location."

"Mmm."

The burger melts in my mouth and the fries are divine. Against my better judgment, I agree to a second round of drinks. They add just the right degree of mellow, and much to my surprise, I pronounce, "I've been thinking about spending the rest of the summer at Fourth Lake."

His brows shoot north as a wide grin dimples his cheeks. "Hey, that's great." Then he looks away for a few seconds and shakes his head. "But I don't think that's such a hot idea."

"Why not? After what went down at the cottage and my confrontation with Fin at the funeral, wouldn't that make me the perfect bait?" I kick myself for giving so much of my plan away.

He reaches across the table gives my hand a squeeze. "No doubt about that. But let's take this bait business slow. Okay?"

He drives me back to Hertz in the Hancock Airport parking garage, pulls next to my rental, and puts his car in park.

I give him my best smile. "Thanks for dinner. It was really great being with you."

When I lean to plant a goodbye kiss on his cheek, he pulls me to him and covers my lips with his.

I gasp, eagerly respond, and then think better of letting the moment get out of control. I don't know Liam Witcher, and I certainly don't know if I can trust him. Still, it's harder than I thought it would be to pull away.

But I manage it. I gently slide out of his arms toward the door.

"Hey there. Don't run away." He pulls me back in his embrace and whispers, "Did I mention you could stay overnight in my guest room?"

"But didn't I tell you I have a guaranteed rez at the Marriott Courtyard?"

"Damn. Guaranteed?"

"Yep."

His lips cover mine again, ending the repartee, and damn it all if I don't sink right back into the moment. When we finally part for the second time, the windows have fogged over.

Witcher chuckles. "Looks like we don't need that heater anymore. Sure you won't take me up on my invite?"

I shake my head. "Sorry, but as I said, that rez is guaranteed."

"Then how about breakfast?"

I hesitate. I should keep Witcher in my inner circle—he's got information I'm going to need. So that's reason enough to have breakfast with him.

I'm just not sure that's the *only* reason I want to.

"You're on," I say, telling myself I'm just acting as a good PI. Don't close any doors on potential evidence. Especially when that evidence might be conveyed by a very attractive man.

"How about nine?"

"See you then."

I'm almost to White Lake when I check my watch to see it's just past noon.

The breakfast with Witcher was, in a word, confusing. The one time I mentioned Aunt Sallie's murder, he got very quiet and changed the subject. Was he just being respectful of his colleagues at the station? Or was there more going on with Liam Witcher than met the eye?

And yet, despite my unsettling suspicions, the force of attraction took over completely as soon as we got back to the car. Even though the weather was frigid, neither of us seemed to mind that we were engaged in public lip-lock for a good twenty minutes in the parking lot.

When my legs began to betray me, I broke the kiss and murmured, "Whoa there, Witcher. We seem to be attracting a small crowd."

He looked behind him, then nodded. "How about Liam? My friends and co-workers call me Witcher and I'm pretty sure we've moved past friendship."

"Yeah. I'm pretty sure we have."

I stepped back. "Guess I better get on the road."

Liam shook my words away. "But I have a much better idea."

"I'm sure you do, but I really do have to go."

I moved away again, hoping the distance between us would clear my head.

He gave me a longing grin. "Chicken."

"Cluck, cluck. That's me."

I opened the door of my rental, slid beneath the wheel, and pulled the door shut. Then I cracked the window just a little, so that he wouldn't try for another kiss. Truth to tell I was still too vulnerable to refuse what he might ask next. He was irresistible ... and this was one man it would be wise to resist.

Liam leaned down and whispered through the narrow opening, "I'm serious about this, Miss Cluck Cluck. You cannot stay at that cottage. Not alone."

"I know, I know. You don't have to twist my arm. I reserved a room at The Woods Inn this morning. And I'll make only midday visits for a few days to test the water, okay?" I don't know how much I believe it myself, but I hope I sound convincing.

"A few days? Not enough. You need protection."

"I'll think it over and give you a call."

"No thinking it over. No moving in there without a bodyguard. Ya hear?"

I start the engine, eager to get away. "We'll see."

As I drive away, I know exactly where I'm headed. And there's nothing that Liam Witcher—or anybody, for that matter—can do about it.

CHAPTER 22

I pass the entrance to Hotanawa to check in to The Woods Inn, then head for the Big M to buy a six-pack of canned sparkling water to go with some of Uncle Aiden's single malt Scotch.

My entrance into the Hotanawa compound goes unnoticed. Though there are a few cars parked in the garage below Holden Cottage, my guess is the "Natawas" who made it up here for the weekend after Aunt Sallie's service are huddled in front of their living room fireplaces. I wouldn't mind if they froze to death.

That's fine by me. I don't have plans to make myself known any time soon—at least not until I feel secure enough to spend the night.

I take the steps down to the deck, hanging onto the wrought-iron railing that has always been a little wobbly, in an effort to balance the load in my left hand of a purse and the six-pack. The stone steps are uneven, making my descent, even without encumbrances, a journey fraught with peril.

The irony of that thought strikes me: peril? I'm back at the scene of a murder. And the murderer is still on the loose.

I'm relieved to see that the yellow crime scene tape is gone. At least there's that.

When I finally reach the deck, I hesitate. My heart rate has doubled. Not from going down the stone steps, a trip I've made at least a thousand times.

I'm afraid. Afraid of what I might find. Afraid of what I won't.

I walk to the railing and lean forward to see if any evidence remains below. Except for several shards from my shattered lemonade glass sparkling on the moss-covered outcropping, there's no sign that a murder has been committed. The narrow sand beach is smooth; the path along the lake shows no signs of having been trampled; nothing is different, even the breeze from the lake and the gentle lap of water against the shore. Serenity reigns.

I take a few deep breaths before crossing the deck to the front door, set down the sparkling water, and spend the next few seconds searching through the cavern I call a purse, until I find the key.

My hand trembles as I try to fit it into the lock. Finally, after my third try, the door swings into the dark and musty living room. I want to step inside but instead, I stand glued to the threshold, pounding heart punctuated by ragged breathing. Somehow, even though I was here just a few days before, everything seems different now. Darker, somehow. Maybe because the police have put the last nail in the coffin, and I really am alone.

What now? Do I pretend nothing has happened? Should I crank open a few windows, and set a fire in the living room fireplace? What then? Explore the place I remember in such detail that I could make my way around it blindfolded? Let's face it: Whomever killed Sallie is still out there. Liam was right. This is no place for me, unprotected and alone.

I hear footsteps behind me. Every part of my body is instantly covered in goosebumps. I reach in my purse for my Beretta. *Damn!* I've left my weapon at the hotel. I was foolish to come here, and now it's going to be too late.

When I turn I almost collide with Frederick Ashton.

He's in his uniform: sharply creased khakis topped by a dark green polo with the Hotanawa arrowheads stitched on the left sleeve and, tucked in its usual spot under one arm, his clipboard.

He doesn't look too much older than I remember except that after fifteen years his distinctive graying mane has turned snow white. He's still the tall, fit man with distinguished features and large blue piercing eyes, only today those eyes are filled with sadness.

DARK LAKE | 99

He gives me a slight formal bow as he extends a bouquet of daisies and ferns arranged in a Mason jar. I can't help but smile. The Hotanawa tradition prevails. Ever since I can remember, Frederick has presented the same welcoming bouquet to every arriving family.

"Miss Armington, how nice to see you. Welcome to Hotanawa."

"My goodness, what a surprise, Frederick. How did you know I was here?"

He smiles. "It's my job."

"Of course it is. How could I forget? Please come in."

"But weren't you on your way out?"

I set my purse on the table and lie. "I was just going to run back to the Big M but that can wait."

When I take the extended bouquet, he says, "Actually, I must confess I didn't know you were here until Artie Curtis told me he saw you at the Big M."

After I motion Frederick to follow me into the living room, I say, "Artie Curtis? Are the same dock boys, er, men still here? It's been such a long time."

"If I recall correctly it's been fifteen years since your unfortunate departure, and many dock boys have come and gone except for Artie, who married one of the maids. Do you remember Eunie? The cute one? Believe it or not they have two children attending Old Forge High School.

"Eunie is in charge of the laundry now and I'm grooming Artie to take my place. He pretty much handles the tasks I no longer care to."

"Well, I hope he's patient. I don't see you retiring any time soon."

After he settles in Uncle Aiden's wing chair by the fireplace, I say, "I suppose you've heard that Aunt Sallie left Holden Cottage to me?"

He nods. "That's why I'm here. I'm sure you have questions."

"I do. But to tell you the truth, I'm not quite ready to move in. I've taken a room at Woods."

His brows arch. "Oh?"

"I need to get someone in to clean. As far as I know, the cottage hasn't been touched since ..."

I see the pain flash in Ashton's eyes and quickly change the subject. "Are all the families in?"

"Just the Napiers so far. But there will be thirty for the Fourth. So sorry—thirty-one counting you. And that's not including guests. I should have a proper head count soon."

Frederick pulls a Montblanc pen from his shirt pocket, then clears his throat several times before saying, "I thought I might take this opportunity to remind you of the compound's many idiosyncrasies. That is, if you have the time."

He stands and hands me an index card headed by his cell number, followed by the numbers for the boat dock, kitchen, and laundry, and then says, "Oh, by the way, I tried ringing you before I came up, but to no avail. Is the phone out of order?"

I stammer, "Uh-uh, that could be. I usually use my cell so I haven't checked it out." I give him my cell number, then say, "I'll call Frontier first thing tomorrow."

"Well, then, let's begin with the finances. Food and beverage costs, including gratuities, will be billed at the end of July and again following inventory week in mid-September.

"The maid service was scheduled in January but, as you might remember, Sallie—uh, uh, your aunt—never used our service. She had Teenie Herold come in every week or so for a touch-up."

I smile, remembering Teenie who came from Big Moose. Teenie was anything but that. All the Herolds were sturdily built and had been working for the Holdens for at least two generations. "Is Teenie still available?"

"I haven't seen her since I arrived, but I know she would do everything in her power to accommodate you. Your aunt must have her number written in that famous book she keeps—uh, kept—in the kitchen.

"Laundry is already set in stone, but there are some late afternoon times open. I'll speak with Eunie about that.

"The daily sign-up sheets for boats are still *de rigeur*."

He gives a derisive sniff. "The families are still very touchy about that. Last weekend one of the Taylor great grandchildren took a boat without signing. Oh my, what a ruckus that caused.

"Cocktail service in the boathouse living room remains the same: not before 5:30 pm except for the Sunday brunches. Would you care to join us this evening? It's the first cook-out of the season, though we're holding it indoors. Just too blasted cold to try the dock."

"No thank you. I plan to keep a low profile for awhile. I'm sure the others will have questions about the— about my aunt."

Ashton slowly shakes his head. "The other families were notified, but outside each sending a member to the funeral, not one single person has asked about the—" He pauses. "It's as if nothing ever happened. Which is, I suppose, the way they want it."

He lets out a deep breath, stares away for a few seconds, and then, with his smile back in place, says, "Whenever you're ready to take dinner in the boathouse, please notify me the morning of that day— and of course, the number of guests you will be expecting."

Ashton checks off the last line on his list. "I think I've covered all my bases. Again, welcome. It's such a pleasure to see you."

When he rises he retrieves a thick envelope from beneath his clipboard and hands it to me.

Aunt Sallie's bold handwriting is unmistakable. The envelope is addressed to Frederick Ashton, NP, Bahamas.

"I received this just before I came north. I have left part of her note to me in the outer envelope."

When he pauses and swallows a couple of times, I notice his eyes are glistening. My heart tugs. I knew the two were close friends, but ...

When Ashton speaks again, his voice is husky with sorrow. "Sallie and I enjoyed a wonderfully close relationship over the years. We shared many good times."

Frederick stops and then says, "If you would burn her letter to me after you read it, I'd be most appreciative of your discretion."

My jaw drops as his words sink in.

When he turns for the door I follow, too stunned to speak.

Again he bows and extends his hand. "I'm at your service any time."

I grab my purse, lock the front door, and practically tromp on Ashton's heels as I follow him up the stone steps.

Ever the gentleman, he precedes me to my rental and opens the door for me. "I hope you'll be moving in soon. It saddens me not to see the cottage lights from my window."

"You'll be the first person I call. I promise."

CHAPTER 23

I wait until I'm in my room at The Woods Inn to open the envelope.

The letter to Frederick Ashton is written on Holden Cottage stationery, the thick creamy sheets engraved at the top with a sketch of the cottage as seen from the lake below.

Dearest Freddy,

It's almost midnight, and I'm sadly experiencing the solitude of Hotanawa as best I can without you. Your call informing me of your delayed arrival was a terrible disappointment, but to hear your voice almost made things right. Please know that I understand your commitment to the other half of your life and know, too, that I am so grateful for the time you give to Hotanawa.

The compound seems to have weathered another harsh Adirondack winter without too much damage to the buildings. There are the usual ice heaves on the roads but nothing that can't be easily repaired upon your arrival.

I hope I'll still be here when you finally do arrive, but unfortunately I might not. In January Arlene took a leave of absence from her job at the Chicago Board of Trade and came to Inlet to move in with that dreadful Fin Holden.

Early last month Fin sans Arlene paid Aiden and me an unannounced visit in Wilmette.

After getting through the barest of amenities, he began quizzing us at length about Holden Cottage and who would inherit at my death.

It soon became clear to both of us that Fin didn't give a whit about Arlene if she wasn't inheriting, but unfortunately, she's so smitten with him she can't see the forest for the trees.

Aiden and I were as pleasant as we could be under the circumstances, but when Fin announced that he and Arlene planned to marry on the Hotanawa dock Fourth of July weekend, and hoped to spend most of the summer at Holden Cottage in the years to come, I took immediate legal steps to insure that Fin Holden will never get his hands on this Cottage.

As you know, I arrived today as scheduled and was shocked to see that my daughter has lost a great deal of weight and is so jumpy and fragmented that I'm sure she's on some sort of drug.

Worse still, we had a huge row over the Cottage and the part in it that Fin as our future son-in-law would play. I ended the row by announcing that if Arlene thought Fin Holden was getting this property she had another thing coming.

Oh, Freddy, I wish you could have seen the look on her face because if looks could kill …

I hate to burden you with this task, Freddy, but if anything untoward should happen to me you must be sure the enclosed gets to my niece, Allie Armington. Surely you remember that darling girl. She was so bright and so full of spunk.

And you must deliver the letter to her personally. I don't trust the mails or that awful Fin Holden.

I plan to post this first thing tomorrow morning.

The bottom half of the third sheet has been torn away. Whatever is missing must not apply to the cottage or to me.

Sallie must have made it to the post office the following morning or I wouldn't be reading this letter now.

What disturbs me most is that Arlene knew Sallie didn't plan to leave Holden Cottage to her.

Still, it's hard to believe that she would personally be involved in her mother's death.

I tear open the envelope.

Dearest Allie,

If you are reading this, I am dead and you are now the sole owner of Holden Cottage. Sad to say your possession of this property is by default, but I could not in all good conscience allow Fin Holden to grab my beloved Holden Cottage through a bogus marriage to Arlene.

Hopefully, once he learns that she has not inherited the Cottage, he'll go his merry way and she'll be free of him at last.

I'm terribly concerned about Arlene. She's much too thin and seems overly anxious and agitated. I can't help but think she's on drugs. If there is anything you can do for her, I'm sure you will. She loves you like a sister and once things shake out, I'm sure your relationship will return to its former lovely state.

I have made financial provisions to insure that the ownership of Holden Cottage will not become a burden to you through the years. You're a wise young woman and one whom I am sure will spend the income judiciously.

All best wishes to you, my darling niece,
Sallie

I carefully fold the letter and place it back in the smaller envelope along with Sallie's rather revealing letter to Frederick Ashton. There's just enough innuendo to raise two questions: Arlene and Fin are at the top of my list of murder suspects, maybe Arlene more than Fin. Both wanted Holden, but were they in this together?

And now, after reading Sallie's letter to Frederick, I can't help but wonder if there was something more between those two? Had June been the perfect month to conduct a secret tryst?

CHAPTER 24

That night I dream about a part of the compound I've never been to. I don't know why, but it emerges on the landscape of my dreams as I sleep. I see myself walking up the exit drive to the highway. For some reason, we kids who traipsed all over Hotanawa and knew every square foot of the compound had never explored this area.

I wake up in a cold sweat. Maybe that exit drive holds the answer to something. Maybe I'll find something I'm looking for.

After my restless night at Woods, I rise, shower, and head for the lobby to bolt a doughnut and a cup of coffee from the station set up for early risers. My plan is simple: Go to the cottage, park, and then walk up the exit drive.

The air is crisp but invigorating as I step out of my rental to climb the rutted road through the dense woods, past a huge moss-covered boulder, and see a small house on my left about twenty yards from, and just out of sight of, Route 28.

No car.

I step onto the creaky porch and knock.

No answer.

An uneasy feeling settles into my stomach. What is this place? I've never been here before, but I can't shake the feeling that I know what I'm going to find—maybe because I saw it so clearly in my dream.

I turn the handle and the door swings inward to reveal a dilapidated couch, worn by years of use, shoved against the opposite wall.

Next to it leans a wrought-iron, single-bulb floor lamp with no shade.

To the left is a small kitchen with a freestanding sink, a four-burner gas stove, and a rickety table surrounded by four well-worn metal folding chairs. There are no dishes or utensils; the wooden shelves nailed in between the bare studs are empty.

Noticing that there are several rotted floorboards with one spot caved in, I carefully cross the living room to a door to the right of the couch and open it. That room, at the most, is ten foot square with a double bed jammed against the wall. Opposite the bed is a door leading to a cramped bath that appears to have been added much later.

Nobody's home and it looks like nobody's been home for a long, long time; but permeating the air is the acrid smell of recently cooked crystal meth.

I step onto the porch, and punch a number into my cell.

When Liam answers, I skip the pleasantries. "I know where they've been cooking. It's on the Hotanawa property. I think it used to be the caretaker's cabin."

"Allie? You're at the cottage? I thought I told you not ..." There's a long pause. "What in hell time is it?"

I check my watch. "I told you I have a room at The Woods Inn. It's just that I couldn't sleep. Sorry. It's six-thirty."

I ignore his low moan. "But this is important," I continue. "Fin never stopped production. Just changed venues. And right under our noses. Please come up. You won't be sorry. I promise."

I cut the connection and continue up the road to the highway. The exit is between two squat telephone pole-sized posts supporting a heavy chain with a substantial padlock.

Just across the highway is a trailhead parking lot. It's not at all unusual for cars to park overnight or even longer at a trailhead since many Adirondack tourists are into camping. All the meth cooks have to do to avoid arousing suspicion is keep changing vehicles.

I squint to make out the writing on the sign across the highway: Rondaxe something or other. What a perfect setup. Park at the trailhead, ferry the equipment and basics across the road late at night when the traffic is sparse. Cook up a few batches and then adios before sunrise.

Could it really be that simple? Are Fin and Arlene so far gone that they murdered Aunt Sallie so they would inherit Holden Cottage? So they could have access to the ideal headquarters to run their illicit operation?

I'm sitting at the picnic table on the deck checking my e-mails on my cell when I hear footsteps on the stone steps and Clarissa Napier appears. I have to force myself to suppress a shudder.

Fifteen years haven't been kind to the gangly, freckled, horse-faced kid I remember. "Clarissa Napier," I say, pocketing my cell. "It's been a long time." And then I lie. "How nice to see you."

When I point to the bench on the other side of the table, she settles on it.

"We are all so sorry about Sallie. What a loss to the community. How are the Armingtons holding up?"

"As well as can be expected. It's been hard on everybody."

"Suicide is always hardest on the survivors."

I fix her with an icy stare. "So is murder."

She pretends not to hear me. "There's a rumor that Holden Cottage went to you. Is that true?"

I nod, sure she's dying for an explanation, but I have no intention of hashing over all the sordid details.

"But we were all so sure that Arlene would ... because, after all, her middle name is Holden."

"I too, was very surprised at Sallie's decision to leave me the cottage, but I'm sure she had her reasons."

Clarissa lets out a conspiratorial breath before she leans closer. "It's rumored that Arlene's on drugs."

"Oh?"

She gives me a knowing smirk and then lobs the first shot across my bow. "It's town gossip that Arlene and Fin Holden had been shacked up at his family's camp since the first of the year. There's even some talk about Arlene being pregnant."

Her statement hangs in the air until I shrug it away. And then she reloads to take a second shot. "It's too bad you're so far away. Houston, isn't it? How ever will you be able to take the time to enjoy Sallie's magnificent gift?"

Before I can think of an answer, Clarissa holds up one hand and chirps, "Not to worry. Our families held a meeting the day after Sallie's funeral, and we've found the perfect solution to your problem. *Annnnd*, since I'm the first to arrive, I've been authorized to make you a proposal."

She gives me a sympathetic smile as she places her hand over her heart. "The families have all agreed that it the only sensible solution to this problem is to relieve you of this burden by purchasing Holden Cottage."

So, that's what these people have in mind! First they convince the police not to investigate Sallie's death lest, God forbid, Hotanawa should get any bad press. And now they want to take away her beloved cottage? No way. *No way in hell!* I might not be up to tackling a move into the cottage right away, but the bitch doesn't know that she's just sealed the deal.

I smile and deftly plant my knife.

"How kind of all of you to worry about me, but the distance will be no problem. No problem at all. I handle most of my business by phone and online. In fact, once I move in, I'm planning to stay here until October."

Clarissa tries to iron away the naked hate that fills her face, but she fails. "October? Really? And may I ask what your business is?"

"I'm a practicing attorney and a certified private investigator."

"How very interesting. Who would have thought ...?" Her voice trails off as she gazes down for a few seconds. When she looks up, her steely eyes betray her next words. "I'm sure everyone in the compound will be delighted to hear the news."

After she stands, she offers, "Why don't you drop by Napier Cottage for a drink around five? The rest of the clan should be arriving by noon. I know they would love to see you after all this time."

In a pig's eye! The Napiers, except for Tommy, who has always been a close friend of my cousin Alan, were never friendly with any of the Armingtons. And now I have every reason to despise these people with every ounce of my being. So I lie.

"Thanks so much for the invitation, but I anticipate an exhausting day ahead of me. How about a rain check?"

She nods, obviously relieved she can report she completed her mission without actually having to suffer my presence over cocktails. "Of course. I'll get back in touch."

Clarissa takes a few steps, then pauses. "By the way, did I mention I'm married? I married Ray Demme. Remember him?"

How could I forget Ray Demme? The Demmes were dear Nantucket friends of the Napiers. Ray is probably ten years my senior, a total jackass, and a professional snob. It has to be a marriage made in heaven.

"And we have two sons."

"How nice for you." I can't help but stir it up a little. "Let's just hope things have returned to normal."

Clarissa's eyebrows arch. "What do you mean, normal?"

"Well, if you promise not to tell anyone I told you ..." I lean in conspiratorially. "Since Sallie's murder, Hotanawa just isn't the same safe haven it used to be."

She frowns and pronounces, "It was suicide. Can't you get that through your head?"

Clarissa takes a deep breath before crooning, "I think everything is ... normal. Actually, I can assure you that everything *is* normal. As you might remember, I'm good friends with Bo Zandt, and he would have told me about anything that wasn't normal."

It's my turn to lob a few shots in Clarissa's direction. "I'd never want to question the authorities, of course. But things around here really seem to have run amuck. You know. Drugs. Murder. Even a drive-by shooting from one of those cigarette boats."

I watch Clarissa for her reaction. She's gotten very still and seems to be concentrating on the line of ants crawling across the deck.

I touch her arm softly and say, "Thank goodness you've got friends on the police force. I'm sure they'll find who's responsible in no time. And then Hotanawa will be just as safe as it always was. Our private paradise, right?"

I'm really enjoying Clarissa's discomfort. She's made her bed—now she has to lie in it.

"Yes," she murmurs, as she turns to go. "Paradise."

My guess is the Hotanawa families would do almost anything to keep their little paradise intact.

And suddenly, I begin to read Clarissa's nervousness a different way. If the families have the ability to control the police ... what else have they managed to hide?

CHAPTER 25

When I hear a car groaning up the hill, I'm torn. It's been less than twenty-four hours since Liam and I parted but it seems like eons. I can't deny that I want to see him—just thinking about his kiss brings an involuntary shudder. How wonderful to be in lust again after such a long, long drought.

But I hardly know Liam, and I can't say I trust him implicitly. Am I playing with fire?

I wait for his footfall on the stone steps. I plan to play it cool, but the instant I see him, the plan disintegrates. I rush across the deck and fall into his arms as his mouth hungrily covers mine.

When we break for air, I pull him over to the picnic table and scoot in beside him.

He tries for another kiss, but I lean back. "First, let's get business out of the way."

He gives me a wicked grin. "But I thought we were dealing with business?"

"This is serious, Liam. Somebody's been cooking meth in the abandoned caretaker's cabin up the driveway. And since there's a big fat 'No Trespassing' sign tacked on one of the posts at the highway, it's my guess that no stranger would stumble into such a convenient situation. Wouldn't someone have to know about this place? Like Fin? Or even ... Clarissa Napier?"

At the mention of Clarissa's name, I see a flash of recognition in

Liam's eyes. Something tells me Liam has more information about the Napiers than he's letting on.

He holds up a cautioning hand. "Something new came to our attention when the snow began to melt in March. Large leaf bags filled with used plastic water bottles, old tubing, dirty gloves, and empty packs of cold medication turned up along the roadsides. They're called 'trash labs.'

"The cooks don't need a permanent setup anymore. Instead they're using the 'one-pot' or 'shake and bake' method to make the meth. It's like meth-making on the go.

"This is catching on so fast that we've just recently designated two patrol cars to do nothing but search the roadsides and pick up evidence. Besides gathering the evidence, we're protecting innocent people who might come across these trash sacks, and pick up a bottle that might explode. Or if they drink the acid, their throats are eaten."

I instinctively put a hand to my throat.

"How awful," I say, shaking my head.

"It is."

❧

Once Liam has inspected the caretaker's cabin, he's all business.

While I lock down the cottage, Liam, seated at the picnic table, cell jammed to his ear, is barking orders to someone on the other end. "I need two men on this 24/7."

He shakes his head. "I know the Fourth is coming up and we'll have a skeleton crew, but this is a live one. I'm positive. Just listen and do what I say. There's a trailhead parking lot just across the highway with a good observation spot about ten feet up the trail into the trees. I tried the binocs and got straight shot. No, no—not with a weapon, surveillance only. I want them brought in alive and kicking. Savvy?"

Whoever is listening must capitulate because a large grin creases his dimples and he says, "Thanks. I owe you a big one."

Liam pockets his cell. "I'm famished. Let's go find food."

After sharing a pizza and an unassuming Chianti on the sun deck of Screamen Eagle, I casually mention something about Clarissa stopping by the cottage.

Liam's eyebrows arch. "She and Ray are down early this year."

"You know her husband?"

"Used to, yeah." He looks a little uncomfortable. "I actually dated Clarissa one summer before she and Ray hooked up."

"Really?"

"Yeah. But the real affair that got tongues waggin' was when Clarissa shacked up with Chief Zandt."

And now it all makes sense. The reason Clarissa is the go-between for the families and Zandt is because she can still work her wiles on the chief.

Frankly, I can't say I see how the horse-faced, freckled Clarissa has any "wiles" at all. Not that I'm being catty.

"You and Clarissa, huh?" I say to Liam. "She doesn't seem like your type."

"What would you know about my type?" He leans close to me and whispers in my ear. "I hear you have etchings in your room at Woods."

"No. That's not the way it goes. You're supposed to ask me up to see *your* etchings."

He gives me a vulpine leer. "Nah. There are new rules."

For a second I let myself be taken over by pure, unadulterated lust. But then the PI part of my brain clicks on, and I realize ... it might not be such a bad way to get Liam to open up to me. I don't know if the guy's on the straight and narrow or on the down low, but if there's any funny stuff going on, he just might give me the info I need.

And if I know anything about men, it's that they're an open book in the bedroom.

"New rules, huh?" I nibble on his ear. "Then how do I play?"

There was little trouble getting Liam up the stairs and into my room. Not a soul was in the Lobby.

I don't think either one of us had planned to immediately fall into bed, but the trail of clothes across the floor spoke volumes.

Though our first encounter slaked our mutual desire, the second played out in slo-mo as we took the time to explore and savor one another.

I find myself desperately rationalizing. Is it possible that such a good lover could be a bad cop?

Now, the late afternoon sun streams across the bed as curtains billow with breeze from the lake. Liam, spooned around me, is purring against my back.

I'm so satisfied, I don't want to move. So I spend a few minutes replaying each move, as I remember how very well the two of us fit together.

But I've got to pull back before I get off track entirely. I'm not here for mind-numbing, unbelievably hot encounters with a near stranger. I'm here to solve a murder.

I ease from his embrace, retrieve my clothes from the floor, and make my way to the bath.

It doesn't take long to shower and spruce up a bit, and with a fresh towel wrapped around me, I return to the bedroom to see Liam on his back, his purr ramped up to a satisfied snore.

I look at his cell phone, hastily discarded on the table.

I wonder if I just ...

But no. He hasn't given me any serious cause to be suspicious. I don't need to go rifling through his personal belongings.

At least not yet.

⚬⚬

It's close to seven when we hit The Laughing Loons Tavern for a drink. Liam downs his Laphroaig in one swift move, then requests another, which arrives along with my "slightly dirty" martini.

"My, my. I didn't know you were a single malt man."

His dimples flashed. "There's a lot you don't know about me. But you'll have plenty of time to find out."

I'm curious about what he means by *There's a lot I don't know.* I also find myself thinking more and more about Clarissa, and the strange little relationship she seems to have forged with Zandt.

And then the last thing he says—*plenty of time to find out*—settles in the pit of my stomach. Does Liam want something serious?

A small rush of guilt intrudes as I realize I might be worse than Clarissa. Am I having a sexual romp with Liam for information, or is there more to it?

I look up at the beautiful pressed tin ceiling for a few seconds, hoping to find the right words. "About this plenty of time thing. I ..."

His hand covers mine. "Hey, if this little thing we have going is just for fun, that's fine by me."

The relief I expected to rush over me is more reluctant to arrive than I thought, but when it finally comes, I relax and take a sip of my martini. "That's great. Just so we're on the same page."

After my second martini and his third Scotch, we decide to stay in the tavern for the food and both order the grilled Angus beef burger and a glass of Chianti.

Our dinner chatter, sprinkled with laughs and knowing looks, is followed by a hurried trip back to my room.

So much for not sleeping with the enemy.

Is Liam the enemy?

Right now, I don't really care.

∽✕∼

Liam's cell vibrating against the wood of the bedside table pulls me from sleep. I open my eyes to see him roll over, grab it, and bring it to his ear. When he speaks into it, his voice is so low that even lying next to him, I can barely make out, "I'm on assignment."

After placing the cell back on the table, Liam rolls to face me and murmurs, "It was nothing. Go back to sleep."

Nice idea, but there's no way I can sleep now. I have two questions I need answered: Who was on the phone and why were they calling at such an odd hour?

Obviously sleep is not a problem with him. He's just beginning to snore when his cell vibrates again and jerks him back to the present.

I turn on the bedside lamp, roll out of bed to head for the bath. Just before I close the door, I hear him say, "I said I'm working. Don't call me again."

In the glare from the bathroom light I see that it's not quite five, a little too early to get up, but getting up is preferable to giving Liam the opportunity to jump my bones yet again.

It's not that I'm having second thoughts about what happened between us. But who's calling him at four-thirty in the morning? Maybe I was right from the beginning: He's got a wife and kids holed up in Utica, and I'm just his latest fling.

Then another possibility intrudes on my consciousness: What if it's not a romantic thing at all? What if Liam's actually working with Fin, not against him? What if that call came from the person who murdered Aunt Sallie?

When there's a knock on the bathroom door I open it to edge past him. "Why don't you shower and dress, then we'll reconnoiter."

He sighs. "What? No questions about those dead-of-night calls? What kind of woman are you?"

I give him a casual shrug. No way in hell I'm going to let him know I'm dying of curiosity. "Business is business, I always say. Let's grab a quick bite here and go back to the cottage."

I pride myself on playing it cool. Of course, on the inside I'm wondering, *Who the hell is this man, and what have I gotten myself into?*

When the shower door closes, I check his cell for recent incoming calls. Blank. All three erased. *Damn. What did I think I would find? The man's a professional.*

CHAPTER 26

My jaw drops when I see that the sliding glass door to the kitchen is wide open. Someone has been in the cottage—someone brazen enough to signal that the cottage's security can easily be breeched.

Liam's voice comes over my shoulder. "As I recall, you locked that door."

"Yes. I did." We ready our weapons and I wait for Liam to precede me into the kitchen.

"You stay put while I check things out, okay?" He gives me a fleeting kiss, then disappears.

I stand there leaning my forehead into the cold hard glass, mind frantically darting from one scenario to the next. Whoever was in the cottage wanted me to know that they could get in anytime they wanted.

Fin? Arlene? Clarissa?

Someone else?

I can't stop shivering. Every fiber of my body warns me to get out of that cottage and make a speedy retreat to the safety of Houston. I don't need to face the sad memory of Sallie lying face down in the lake, or Arlene's sudden alliance with Fin. I'll sell the cottage to the damned "Natawas." Let them deal with Sallie's ghost and the trespassers.

It's then I realize that Liam has returned and his body is gently pressed against mine, offering much-needed warmth. For a second, I relax into him. Then I come to my senses. I'd love someone to lean on, but it seems more apparent than ever that there's no one I can trust.

I pull away from Liam and begin pacing as I gather my wits.

"I'm sure you have work to do," I say curtly. "Better take me back to The Woods Inn and get on with it."

His face crumbles. "You want me to leave? Now?"

I give him my best smile. "It's been great to be with you. But I don't want to keep you from your job. After all, we each have our separate lives."

Liam gives me a mock frown. "If I didn't have a meeting this afternoon that can't be missed, you'd have hell un-embedding me from this area of operations."

He brightens. "How about the fireworks in Old Forge on the Fourth?" He checks his cell calendar and nods. "Yeah. I can easily make it back up here way before that happens. We could make a very nice long weekend out of the Fourth while I keep my eye on the cabin. Whadaya say?"

∽✕∾

I shake my head and hedge. "Not gonna work. As you can see, I'm not quite ready to make the move into the cottage. And if you come back to Woods, I'll have to rent a suite."

"Man, you really know how to hurt a guy's feelings."

I shrug, trying to play it cool. The truth is, I really do want to see Liam again. I'm just not sure I should. "Oh, damn. I forgot one important thing. It'll just take me a few seconds to get it."

After discovering that Aunt Sallie's notebook is not in the drawer where I left it, I frantically paw through the three other kitchen drawers. My initial panic dies when I discover it underneath some gardening tools in the bottom drawer.

Liam's "Hey, time's a-wastin'," filters through my confusion and after I shove the book into my purse, I lock up and climb the stone steps to the cottage parking area.

When he turns to initiate another kiss, I gently push him away.

"No public display. After all, I have my reputation to consider."

He gives me a wicked grin. "If those uptight idiots down the hill had the slightest inkling about what you can do to a helpless guy like me, they'd have you arrested for lewd and lascivious behavior."

The joke lands flat, because I'm reminded of the questionable connection the uptight idiots have with the authorities ... and maybe with Liam himself.

At that, I decide not to tell him about the "traveling" book until I can figure out exactly where he belongs in this scenario.

When I don't react to Liam's lame joke, his grin fades to serious. "I know I don't have to tell you this, but if I don't and something happened to you ... look, and I mean this, Allie, don't even think about coming back here alone. Hear me?"

I want to take his warning in good faith and believe that he's genuinely concerned for my safety. But instead I find myself wondering: What is he trying to hide?

"Sure," I say, with no intention of obeying. "Loud and clear."

∾✕∾

Once I'm back in my room at Woods, I take the easy chair by the window and retrieve Aunt Sallie's book from my purse. I have no intention of heeding Liam's advice and staying away from the cottage. But I wouldn't mind some reinforcements of a different nature.

I open the cover to see Aunt Sallie's bold handwriting: "IMPORTANT THINGS. This book is the sole property of Sallie Armington and should not leave this kitchen!"

I choke back the tears remembering what fun we two used to have as I helped her prep for a meal. Lunch was on the deck, weather permitting.

Sallie used large, round, straw trays to transport the sandwich makings to the long wooden picnic table. Always the lemonade. Always some kind of cookie.

I flip through the time-worn pages divided by food-stained recipes cut from newspapers and magazines, mingled with scraps of paper filled with lists of housekeeping details, to find Teenie Herold's number.

After a few rings, Teenie's familiar voice answers. She expresses surprise when I tell her who I am and that I now own Holden Cottage. Then she offers the expected condolences, ending with, "Glad you have it, but I can't help but feel sorry for Arlene."

I agree with her, but decide not to go into Arlene's tragedy. No reason to add to the gossip.

Instead, in the next five minutes I have engaged her to clean the cottage every Thursday until I close up in the fall.

I tell her that I'm staying at Woods and have no idea how long I will continue to do so, but I assure her I'll be at the cottage when she arrives.

If I'm going back, at least I don't have to go back alone.

When ringing pierces through the warmth of my cocoon, I mutter to no one in particular, "Go away. Try me later."

But the ringing persists until I slide a hand from beneath the blanket to grab my cell.

"Yes?"

Uncle Aiden's voice is filled with panic. "Thank God you answered. I tried the cottage a couple of times, then remembered you said to call your cell."

I hear him inhale and then his breathless, "Is Arlene with you?"

I groggily shake my head. "I haven't seen her since I left Wilmette. Why do you ask?"

There's a yawning silence, then, "She's gone."

That gets my attention. "Gone? Where?"

"Yesterday afternoon. When Ms. Stetson took the first break-day since Sis returned home.

"I made the usual pot of afternoon coffee only to find we had run out of half and half. So I drove over to Family Pantry to pick some up while Sis was taking her nap. I'm positive I was away less than fifteen minutes.

"I thought I'd let her be until Ms. Stetson returned. When Myra did arrive, I poured both of us a glass of wine, then called up the stairs. There was no answer. We both went up. The bed hadn't been touched."

"Why didn't you call me yesterday?"

He either doesn't hear my question or is too wrapped up in the saga to answer. "We thought she might have taken a walk over to Gilson Park. She's been doing that most every afternoon for the past week. Seemed to enjoy going out on a jaunt by herself."

He sighs. "Myra was very pleased. Said it was a sure sign of Sis's progress. Now she's not so sure it was such a good idea. Frankly, we wanted to give Sis a chance to come in on her own before sounding the alarm. I know it's early, but I waited as long as I could."

"It's okay." I pause a few seconds to pull myself into PI mode. "Did Arlene have access to cash or credit cards?"

"Her cards are locked in my desk drawer and I've finally gotten control of the bank accounts. Everything is fine in that department. Apparently, even if Fin tried, he couldn't have gotten to them. As for cash, she could have had some stashed in her room, but not more than a couple hundred at the most."

"What about her cell?"

"She hasn't had access since she went to detox."

"What about the land line?"

"Myra says it'll take a few days but the police can find out about the outgoing calls. But by then ..." His voice fades.

"And you can't report her missing until this afternoon."

"Yes. Yes. Myra told me about the twenty-four hours, but ..."

"Check things out in her room. You know, missing suitcases, clothing, et cetera. But before you do, you need to get some latex gloves. There may be fingerprints and you don't want to compromise the scene."

Another long silence before Aiden's weary voice says, "Okay. Yes. I'll do that right away."

"But with the gloves, okay? Keep in touch. My cell is the best way to contact me."

I hang up and stare at the now silent instrument that pulled me into the gray light of dawn, trying to make sense out of what I have just heard.

Arlene is missing. Has been for ... I squint at my watch. Almost

5:30. Plus or minus twelve hours—plenty of time to fly, or drive, or be driven to Hotanawa. I'm pretty sure that she's headed in this direction. The question is: on or in what and with whom? From what I can gather, Fin isn't in the loop. But if Arlene is angry, there's no telling what might happen.

Maybe I should bring Liam into the loop. But I'm wary of Liam. I spent half the night missing the warmth of his body. I spent the other half wondering why he's so insistent I stay away from Holden Cottage unless he's around to babysit.

I shake the thought away. If Arlene is headed my way, then the best thing I can do is prepare to talk to her face to face, like a human being. Anyway, this is my cousin, my friend. In my heart I know she's not a cold-blooded murderer. Surely not even meth can make a person change that much.

It's almost eleven when I finally crawl out of bed and head for the shower.

After grabbing a bite in the dining room, I crank up my rental and head for the compound. After all, I'm a big girl who's packing heat. And nobody's gonna pick on me in broad daylight. Just let them try.

Besides, if Arlene is on her way, I figure she'll head for the cottage and I better be there to meet her.

When I pull in the main gate and drive past the tennis courts, no one seems to be stirring in the compound. But then, it's early afternoon. Too cool to be on the dock; too early for afternoon tennis.

I pull into the parking lot across from the cottage and descend the stone steps to the deck. To my relief, the sliding glass door to the kitchen is shut.

Once I start a fire in the living room, I crank up the oven in the kitchen and, for some reason, turn toward the glass door.

Icy shards tumble down my spine when I see the lock is open. This means someone has been in here. Are they still?

I pull out my Beretta and take the safety off. Then, for the next fifteen minutes, I go into search-mode as I cover the first floor of the cottage room by room, then cross the walkway to the master bedroom.

It's when I open the door that I realize I've never been in Aunt Sallie's bedroom. But then I wasn't her child, and was never invited to visit her inner sanctum.

Unlike the rest of the rooms in the cottage that have the studs exposed, the walls of this room are beadboard paneling and probably have some kind of insulation behind that.

The bedroom has no windows facing the rest of the house, but on the lake side, across from the king-size bed that is neatly made, there are five tall windows that overlook the water.

I move to the bathroom, which turns out to be almost as large as the bedroom and paneled in beadboard as well. A footed bathtub and a narrow metal step-in shower covered by a frayed and faded curtain are on the right side of a freestanding sink. Beyond that are two small closets. All bear the stamp: turn-of-the-century.

Satisfied that there is no breech in this area, I climb the stairs to find that the second story is empty as well. And then, after opening a couple of windows in each of the four bedrooms, I return to the cozy kitchen and settle at the table. Finally satisfied that whoever was in the cottage is long gone, I pocket my weapon.

I must nod off because the next thing I know, a distant rumble pulls me awake to a darkening sky. I can't believe I fell asleep. I feel so exposed—like someone might have seen me sleeping, and then relished their power to turn around and walk away.

It's nearly four-thirty and still no Arlene.

When the thunder rolls again, I realize the storm is fast approaching and head for the master suite to shut the bedroom windows before heading back to the main house.

I've just stepped back onto the cross walk when the squall line hits and buffets me against the railings as I lurch toward the living room.

Once there I slam down the windows facing the lake, then tend to those above the kitchen sink.

Finally, after shutting the just-opened windows in the four upstairs bedrooms, I make it back to the kitchen just as the first drops spatter on the deck.

The drops morph into a deafening downpour, punctuated with jagged lightning flashes closely followed by claps of thunder.

I cower in the relative safety of the landing above the back hallway as the storm stomps past, heads toward Inlet, and finally fades in the distance.

When the rain stops, I grab a bottle of single malt to soothe my nerves. I've just settled at the kitchen table and taken a swig of Scotch when the wall phone begins to ring. I jump at the ring, then realize Frontier has done its job. The line's been fixed.

Poor Uncle Aiden sounds so weary. "I've been trying your cell for the last fifteen minutes. You told me that was the number to call."

"Sorry. There was a storm and I've been contending with windows. Any news?"

He lets out a long sigh. "One piece of bad news. A small bag is missing. Big enough to carry a few essentials. We thought you might have heard something by now."

"Nothing so far, but I'm pretty sure Arlene will head for the compound."

"Why do you say that?"

"Where else does she have to go?"

There's a long pause, then Myra Stetson comes on the phone. "This is very serious, Allie. Up until yesterday afternoon I thought we were home free, but even with her remarkable progress Sis is still very ragged around the edges.

"Now that I think about it, she may have been meeting Fin. I know you mentioned that possibility before. And if he's with her ... I'm afraid if she gets hold of ... well, even if we were to find her today, it's back to square one. And each time it gets much, much harder to rehab than the last."

"Oh, I get it. More than you might know."

I hang up, sink into the kitchen chair, and drain the glass filled with my drug of choice, then head for my rental car. I can't stay in the cottage any longer. Not tonight.

CHAPTER 28

The following morning, after downing a mug of coffee and scarfing one of Woods' free bear claws, I return to my hotel room to make a list of chores for Teenie Herold.

I then gather my personal things, cram them into a borrowed hotel pillowcase, and make it to the cottage just in time to greet Teenie.

After we exchange hugs and greetings, I give Teenie the list. "Guess you know where everything is?"

She sighs. "I can do this blindfolded."

I'm grateful to have someone else in the cottage. It makes it significantly less creepy. After sending Teenie to strip the bed in the master suite, I go the linen closet on the second floor to check the inventory. The sheets are frayed and the towels have started to unravel along the edges. My best guess is that the linens are at least as old as I am.

Teenie is stripping the bed when I enter the master bedroom. "Don't bother to make the beds this week. I'm going online to order all new linens."

She drops the top sheet on the floor and gives me a pained look. "And you expect me to wash them all?"

"Well, eventually. But not all at once. I don't know when I plan to move in, but I'll let you know in plenty of time."

Teenie gives me a knowing look. "Sorta spooky, ain't it? I mean knowing Miz A was murdered right here in this cottage?"

I give an involuntary shudder. Then I freeze. Teenie must've heard the news from the other families ... so how did she know the truth?

"How did you know she—?"

"Please," Teenie says, with a dismissive wave of her hand. "I've known Miz A for as long as I can remember. That woman would never have taken her own life, come hell or high water."

I have an overwhelming desire to give Teenie a hug. She knew there'd been a murder, and she still agreed to come. I don't have the heart to tell her about the break-ins. That kind of news might really set her off. Instead I nod. "It's so sad she had to die here. She loved this place so much."

Teenie lets out a long sigh. "God rest her sweet soul, poor lady. I really miss her."

"Me too."

We stand staring at each other until I say, "Not to change the subject, but if you like, you can take all the linens that are in the closet home with you and make rags out of them."

At that Teenie shrugs. "Fine by me. I wish Miz A had done that years ago. Everything in that closet is just short of disintegrating."

I hang around until Teenie, laden with the old linens, heads up the steps and drives away.

Since it's mid-afternoon and the sun is warm, I settle on the deck to read Frederick Ashton's one-page newsletter announcing that the holiday activities will crank up Friday the third. The schedule includes times for the Hotanawa sailing regatta, waterskiing competition, and swim meet; and notes that the prizes will be awarded at the picnic held on the boathouse deck and dock.

I won't be joining in those festivities this Fourth. You couldn't pay me enough to hobnob with the families who've tarnished my Aunt Sallie's name to preserve their own. Instead, I've decided that The Woods Inn will be the site of my weekend celebration.

Once again, I have the eerie feeling that someone is watching my movements. I pull my jacket closer around my shoulders and cast a furtive look behind me. Maybe Liam is right; I shouldn't be at the cottage alone.

I know Arlene doesn't have a key, but I'm positive someone else does. Someone has been here, moving things around. Someone wants me to know that they've been here, that they're watching, and that they hold all the power.

Someone I'm not quite ready to reckon with. Not just yet.

CHAPTER 29

Nearly three days after Arlene's disappearance, there hasn't been one word from her.

The Chicago Armingtons are in a panic because, though the police are on it, no one has a clue where to start the search.

To his credit, Uncle Aiden has finally given up calling my cell every hour on the hour since I've assured him that if Arlene should appear, I'll call him immediately. But each time I hang up, I feel helpless and depressed.

My routine has become rote. I rise, hit the lobby for coffee and a bear claw, and then, after tending to what little business I currently have by computer and cell, I make my way to the cottage around noon. There I continue to map out what could have happened to Sallie that fateful morning—the people in her life who might have wanted her dead. I have a growing list of suspects, but not a lot of clues.

Except for the ones accruing in the cottage itself. Every day I come in, things seem a little different. It's almost unnoticeable, but I'm trained to notice subtle changes. Sometimes the kitchen utensils have been rearranged. Or one of the photographs seems to have fallen off the wall. Or I'm sure I left that pad of paper on the left side of the sink, not the right.

I can't shake the unnerving feeling that someone is coming into the cottage every night after I leave and moving things around, ever so slightly. Why? To let me know they can do anything they want. To let me know they don't intend to go away, and that maybe I should.

And yet, I keep going back. By day, the cottage doesn't seem so scary. On the fourth day, the weather decides that it should be summer. The day arrives blue-skied, warm, and blessedly serene. I take advantage of the balmy temperatures by putting on my swimsuit and sunning myself on the deck overlooking the lake. I look out below and can't help but notice the empty dock. I smile.

Just because I'm in pursuit of a murderer doesn't mean I can't take an afternoon off every now and then.

Sunglasses perched above my forehead, with a towel and sun block clutched in one hand, and a juicy summer read in the other, I head down to the lake.

I take the last set of steps down to the dock just as Frederick Ashton steps from the shade of the boathouse to welcome me saying, "Ahhh, I thought I might see you down here today."

He ushers me to a lounge and once I'm settled, he smiles. "I must say, things have gone swimmingly this summer so far. The teens have kept the booze abuse to a minimum; and thankfully, there are no Holdens. Fin always was a handful, but Emery, my favorite of the two, changed for the worse after his time in Iraq. He went in with the first wave, did two tours, then got a medical discharge. I hear it was post traumatic stress."

I nod. "Yes, I remember Emery was the quiet Holden, I'm so sorry to hear he's changed. Was there some sort of fight?"

"Oh yes, and a nasty one at that. The way I heard it: Brent Napier made some kind of comment about the war and how he had proof that 'W' had lied about the WMDs. Of course Emery defended his president and the argument elevated until Emery threw a punch. Then Fin jumped in. By the time it was over both Napier boys got the worst of it. Brent's nose was broken and two of Tommy's ribs were severely bruised.

"The families held a meeting afterward and decided the Holden brothers would be no longer welcome guests at Hotanawa."

I feel a small push of hope at those words. If Fin Holden isn't around, Arlene just might be okay.

I sigh to myself. The situation is getting grimmer by the minute. In most disappearances like this, no news is bad news.

Thinking of Arlene draws my attention to the subject of the cabin in the woods, and I say, "Frederick, what you know about that little cabin at the top of the hill behind Holden Cottage?"

To my mind it's a reasonable question, so I'm surprised at Frederick's initial reaction.

His eyes narrow only for an instant, but even though the squint quickly fades, I can tell his thoughts are in fast forward.

"The little cabin?" After a few seconds, his eyes light with the proverbial "bingo."

"You must mean the cabin near the highway that used to be the caretaker's place.

"As you might already know, the Holden Cottage drive was once the designated exit for the compound; but it hasn't been used as such since the early seventies. Actually, I haven't been up that drive in eons."

Wondering why he needs to qualify his last statement, I plunge on. "I happened up that way a couple of days ago. It's too bad that it's gone to pot."

He stares at me for a few seconds, his mouth slightly open, before replying with a slow, "Yessss. Too bad indeed."

He takes a step toward the boathouse, then pauses. "I hope you didn't go inside. The floors are badly rotted in places. Not safe. Not safe at all, I'd say."

That gets my attention. How would Frederick know about the condition of the floors if he hadn't been there in "eons"?

When I see that he's waiting for my reply, I lower my eyes to the book peeking from beneath my towel.

Finally, after shifting from one foot to the other, he says, "Well, duty calls. I'll be on my way. So glad you're enjoying the day."

I return to the cottage and, realizing that there's been no call from Uncle Aiden, I dial his number. When his voice message plays, I say that there have been no Arlene sightings and hang up.

It's nearly two o'clock and I'm starving, and a tuna sandwich seems the perfect lunch. But there's no tuna to be found and not one can of Diet Coke in either the fridge or the pantry.

That can't be right. On my last trip to the Big M I distinctly remember buying four large cans of albacore in water when I bought the pretzels and the saltines, along with a twelve-pack of Diet Coke.

And then yesterday, when I headed for the kitchen to get the unopened box of pretzels, I had checked the shelves twice before coming up empty, then unhappily resorted to opening the new tin of saltines.

Then it suddenly dawns. Not only are objects being moved, but my food has been disappearing too!

I immediately rule out Teenie Herold since she had been here on Thursday, the day I made my last trip to the Big M.

Then I paw through the fridge for the Swiss cheese and peppered ham. Damn. Not a scrap to be found.

Tingles surf the nape of my neck. Moving things around is one thing. But by taking my food, someone is deliberately messing with me and my personal property. They don't just want to prove that they have easy access to the cottage: They want to prove that they have easy access to *me*.

For reasons not entirely clear to me, I call Liam from the wall phone.

When he answers his cell, I give him the list of missing items, then stop in mid-sentence when I realize that it could be Arlene. Then I blurt out, "Maybe it's Arlene. Maybe she's holed up in the cabin at the top of the hill."

"Don't jump to any major conclusions, okay?" he says. "I can assure you Arlene and Fin have not been sighted at the cabin. Actually, nobody has."

How does he know?

After a long pause he says, "FYI, I'm just up the road, and if you ask me real nice, I can be there in ten minutes."

CHAPTER 30

A bare ten minutes pass before I hear the car and then Liam's familiar footfall on the stone steps. He's carrying a large Big M paper bag.

"You are so busted."

"How else was I going to get your attention?" he says playfully, reaching for me.

I back out of his reach. I don't know whether to be flattered or infuriated. Liam has been coming into the cottage and stealing my food. Why? To scare me? To try and teach me a lesson?

"But, how did you get in here—and when?"

"You come up here about ten or so and leave before dark. Piece of cake."

So Liam's been keeping tabs on me. But why didn't he make his presence known? The whole thing makes my hair stand on end. If he has nothing to hide, then why is he acting so suspicious?

Then it hits me: Could Liam be part of the duo who offed Sallie? Could he also be looking for the tiara? Is that why he's taken such an interest in this case ... and in me?

I quickly push those thoughts out of my mind and change the subject. "So, no Arlene or Fin?"

He's close to me again. He presses his body against mine and murmurs, "I'm so glad you finally called. It's like I've been crawling through the desert for a hundred days and just found an oasis,"

I give in to my own desires, but still, I can't help but wonder what kind of oasis he means.

꘎

We're in the master bedroom on the king-size bed, on top of the new sheets I just purchased online. Liam is passed out from exhaustion. I feel energized. All the questions that have been brewing for the last few days pour forward. Where is Arlene? With Fin? With her baby girl? Or is she somewhere nearby, tantalizingly within reach?

I carefully extract myself from the bed. Liam is fast asleep, snoring.

I haven't been to the caretaker's cabin in days. But after ruminating on my brief but strange interaction with Frederick, it's exactly where I want to go.

I quietly pull on my jeans and head out of the cottage and up the exit road.

Outside the cabin, I have an odd sense of foreboding that rushes through me like a winter wind. Maybe it was a mistake, coming here alone.

I put my hand on the doorknob. It feels warm, as if somebody just touched it.

I push it open.

There, on the couch, is a sight that nothing could have prepared me for.

It's Arlene.

She's dead.

꘎

I hear someone sobbing, then feel my shoulders heave and realize that it's me. I don't know how long I've been sobbing beside her body when I feel a hand on my shoulder. It's Liam.

"I'm so sorry, Allie," he says. "So sorry."

Everything that happens next is a blur. The authorities come, ask me questions, then they put her in a body bag. Through it all, I'm vaguely aware of what they're saying.

She died from an overdose. She tried injecting, which was brutal.

The sores. The infection. There's no ID, just a few hundred-dollar bills on the table next to the couch. When they ask me to identify the body, somehow I do.

Liam escorts me back to the cottage and stays by my side every minute. I call Aiden and thank God when Myra Stetson answers. She gasps at my sad news, then offers to call Ardythe first and then ask the doc for meds.

A couple hours later, when Myra and I talk again, she says, "I don't know how much good the sedation will do. This just might kill him. First his wife, and now Arlene.

"I'm so sorry, I really thought I could win this one. Arlene was so bright, but then so very angry. That was the stumbling block. She had to get past that anger before ..."

Her voice fades, then she says, "Your uncle will be needing your dad. Will you make that call for me?"

I finally manage to blurt my answer. "Of course. Don't give it another thought."

I hang up and look at Liam. At this point, I have no energy to question his intentions. Numbly, I let him take me in his arms.

CHAPTER 31

When we arrive in Wilmette the following afternoon, Arlene's body is sent to a crematorium in nearby Skokie. Thank heavens Liam asked if he could accompany me on the trip, and I was too weak to say no.

When we enter the front hall, I see Myra first. She's visibly shaken. She gives me a brief hug, then asks me to come to her room.

Once there, she shows me the note Arlene had hidden before she ran away, and asks me to read it before she shows it to the family.

After she hands me an unaddressed envelope, she walks over to the window that faces the lake.

I open the note. Even though it's barely more than a few scribbled lines, I can tell it's Arlene's handwriting:

I'm sorry about Mama. I'm sorry about Fin. I'm sorry about the drugs. Burn me. I'm going to Hell.

There is no signature.

I walk over to join Myra. "You interpreted the 'burn me' to mean she wanted to be cremated?"

Shock crams her face. "Did I do wrong?"

I let out a sigh. "It is what it is. If Uncle Aiden or the sibs don't object, then I guess it's fine by me."

I raise the note. "Who else knows about this?"

She shakes her head. "Just the two of us. No one seemed to be able to make a decision about the service or the burial, so when I found it this morning ..."

She sees the question in my eyes and adds, "I was packing my things, and when I cleaned out the bottom drawer, I found it under my sweats."

She points to the page. "What do you think the first two sentences mean?"

I shrug. "It doesn't really matter now, does it? She's dead."

I wait a few seconds, then ask, "Did Arlene ever discuss what happened to her mother in the sessions at Hazelden?"

"Not when I was with her. Actually, she hardly ever mentioned Mrs. Armington."

I can't help but feel like we've reached a dead end. If Arlene *did* have something to do with Sallie's murder, we'll never find out about it now.

"When you told Uncle Aiden about Arlene's wish to be cremated, did you tell him there was a note?"

She blushes and shakes her head. "I wanted someone from the family to see it first. Ardythe was totally unglued and Alan is still en route. And poor Mr. Armington, what with the TIA and all, I just couldn't burden him."

TIA: transient ischemic attack; medical-ese for a so-called ministroke. "He's had a TIA? How bad is it?"

"His left side is slightly impaired but the doctor says he just needs to rest. He should be just fine with time."

She looks down at the note I'm holding and then at me. "What do you think?"

I begin tearing the note into tiny pieces. "This is what I think."

She smiles, her eyes glistening. "That's what I think, too."

⁓

It's Friday and I'm standing second in the pew, thankful that my mother was too grief-stricken to come. Yes, the same "grief-stricken" woman who had questioned Arlene's "persuasion" and made snide comments about her weight.

My father is on the aisle and Liam stands staunchly to my left, clasping my hand in his. For the moment, I let him.

As before, the other Armingtons command the front pew. But this time Aiden, still suffering from the effects of the TIA, is slumped in a wheelchair parked in front of the first pew. On the aisle, in a steel folding chair, sits Alan, who just arrived from Hong Kong this morning, leaving his family behind for a second time. On Aiden's other side is Myra Stetson, who for the present is acting as his "nurse," thanks to Ardythe's persuasive begging.

The first pew now holds only four. Ardythe is on the aisle, but leaning heavily against her husband Doug. Their two sons, Geoff and Sam, stand next to him.

And then there's the issue of Arlene's real or imagined baby. For some reason there was no autopsy before the cremation and therefore no confirmation of a pregnancy. Since there's no proof, the only person who knows the truth is Fin. And he's nowhere to be found. Damn his eyes!

There are no pallbearers. No visiting "Natawas." No flower-covered casket. And, of course, no Fin. And then there's the issue of Arlene's real or imagined baby. For some reason there was no autopsy before the cremation and therefore no confirmation of a pregnancy. Since there's no proof, the only person who knows the truth is Fin. And he's nowhere to be found. Damn his eyes!

The organ drones out "The Church's One Foundation" as the Episcopal priest enters and comes to stand before the half-filled church.

He begins reading from The Burial of the Dead: Rite One. "I am the resurrection and the life, saith the Lord ..."

His voice fades as I remember the treasured times Arlene and I had shared.

Echoes of children screaming: "Olly, Olly, Ox" at the tops of their lungs. Salamanders trapped in a jar. Baby ducks. Wiggly garter snakes.

"Psalm One Hundred Twenty-one," the priest announces. "I will lift up mine eyes unto the hills."

"You're it!"

"Am not!"

"Are too!"

"Am NOT!"

"The Holy Gospel of our Lord Jesus Christ according to John."

"It's my turn to wear the tiara first!"

"No, it's mine!"

"The Twenty-third Psalm is found on page ..."

"Fin kissed you? Oh, gosh, Allie! I wish he would kiss me too! Tell me everything! How did it feel? Did he stick his tongue in your mouth? What did you do next? Oh, please, Allie. Don't leave anything out!"

"And now, for The Lord's Prayer. Please turn to ..."

"I wanted you and Momma to be the first to know. Fin and I are getting married. I had his baby in March."

"Into thy hands, O merciful Savior, we commend Thy faithful servant Arlene Holden Armington." Amen.

"I'm doing only a few lines a day. Fin wants me thin for the wedding."

And then the funeral is over.

"Let us go forth in the name of Christ."

CHAPTER 32

I'm standing in the Armingtons' living room mingling with the few mourners who came to offer condolences to Uncle Aiden, who is sitting in his wheelchair near the fireplace. Everyone is treating me with a strange mix of respect and horror. It takes me a while to realize that they all must know I'm the one who found the body.

For some reason I keep waiting to hear the hum of Fin's motorized contraption, but there is none. The bastard. He didn't have the guts to appear at his fiancée's service, or own up to the fact that he and Arlene share a child. Now I hate him with all my heart.

Myra Stetson has just brought Aiden a steaming mug of coffee. I check my watch and smile to myself. It's exactly 4:30, Uncle Aiden's coffee time. Even though Myra's been at the house only a few weeks, she's easily accommodating his peculiar habits.

My father's arm circles my shoulder and pulls me to him, so that he can plant a kiss on my cheek.

"I like your young man."

We both turn to see Liam and Alan deep in conversation by the open French doors, watch as both take a swig of beer, laugh spontaneously, then glance sheepishly at us before stepping out of sight onto the porch.

Alan is an excellent judge of character. Surely if Alan likes Liam, he couldn't be a bad man.

I look up at Dad. "Do you remember him?"

"Not really. There were lots of kids around back then. To tell you the truth, I didn't even recognize the man."

"Neither did I. He was sorta dorky back then. Now he's the consummate good cop." In my mind I add, *at least I hope he is.*

"I'm glad your mother isn't here," Dad says. "If you recall, she didn't think too much of you and Mr. Cotton staying at the Deer Path after Angela's wedding."

When he realizes that his mention of my dead fiancé might open old wounds, he murmurs, "Please forgive me. I wasn't thinking."

I pat his arm. "Hey, Dad, it's okay. It should be pretty obvious that I've moved on."

I change the subject. "Did you notice that Myra Stetson seems to have become part of the family?"

"Only because Ardythe begged her to stay until poor Aiden is fully recovered. He needs special attention."

Liam appears. "Ready to head out?"

My father smiles up at him. "Nice to see you again after all these years, son." My dad wags a finger in Liam's face. "You better take good care of my daughter or you'll be hearing from me."

⚬⚬⚬

Gentle, tender sex is a healing balm for pain and sorrow, and Liam seems to know that's exactly what I need. Now, cuddled in the warmth of his arms, I feel completely content. Whether or not I feel completely safe remains to be seen.

When I wake up, I'm alone. I sit up to see the blue reflection and hear the low hum of the TV coming through the door to the living room, and pull the sheet from the bed to wrap around me.

Liam is slumped in one of the two large club chairs in front of the tube, with a large hotel bath towel knotted at his waist.

He's talking on his cell, but clicks off the second he sees me. "I have to take the first flight to Syracuse tomorrow."

This is unsettling news. The news itself isn't so bad, but the strange way Liam hung up the phone makes me suspicious. "I can't quite do that. Dad's still here. I should wait to go when he does."

"Gotcha. Just let me know when you'll be back."

Then he smiles, at ease once again. "Hungry?"

We finish the evening with a late, late supper of smoked salmon washed down with a nice bottle of Veuve Clicquot.

Our parting clinch at the airport lasts until a traffic cop knocks on the window and tells us to wrap it up and move along.

What's he heading back to so fast?

I'm not sure, but I have half a mind to find out.

CHAPTER 33

As it turns out, I'm making the trip back to Fourth Lake alone. Liam has been called to a meeting in Albany and isn't sure when he can join me.

I didn't get Liam's message until I landed in Syracuse and the flight attendant gave the passengers permission to use our cells.

With each of his words, the stone in my stomach grows. "Looks like it might not be for a couple of days. Something big is up. That means I won't be communicating with you until this operation is over. I'm sorry, but you better get used to sudden calls, long absences, and late nights. It's the nature of the business."

He pauses, then says, "And, I hate to keep harping on this, but please don't move into Holden Cottage until I get off this assignment."

The abrupt change in his tone—now cold, businesslike, and domineering—is a bit jarring. Let it go, Allie, I tell myself. He's just doing his job.

The day is warm and sunny and the drive from Syracuse to Inlet is an easy one. It's late afternoon by the time I stop at the Big M. My plan is to replenish the cottage pantry, re-stock the fridge, and have a nice home-cooked dinner before going to The Woods Inn for the night.

After trundling five sacks down the stone steps and unpacking them, I treat myself to a drink from Uncle Aiden's dwindling supply of single malt Scotch.

Half an hour later, I plate the pan-seared filet mignon and fresh ear of Silver Queen corn and open a nice Pinot Noir. Because the weather is unusually mellow, I take my dinner to the deck where I can watch the sunset and the stars begin to pop.

Arlene is gone, and now there's no way to find out what really happened between her and Sallie. Fin was nowhere to be seen in Wilmette. Does that mean he's back at the compound?

Now that more of the families have trickled in for the summer, it feels less frightening to be at the cottage alone. But then I remind myself that the families are not to be trusted, either. No one is.

It's well after ten by the time I've cleaned up and secured the cottage. I look over my shoulder in the direction of the cabin as I walk away, trying to get the image of Arlene's dead body out of my mind.

On a whim, I go back inside the cottage and tuck one of Aiden's bottles of Scotch into my purse. Then I head for The Woods Inn for yet another long night.

⌘

The next morning, after a long, hot shower, I pull on jeans and a tee, and make my way to the lobby to cadge my usual breakfast fare.

The three-minute drive from The Woods Inn to the cottage has become rote but when I open the door to the living room, I let out a surprised gasp.

Chaos reigns. Cushions tossed to the floor; drawers flung open; even the half-empty Scotch bottles and bar glasses on the commode have been turned on their sides. The commode's door hangs on one twisted hinge, and the cocktail napkins and bar tools have been pulled from the shelves and scattered on the floor.

I grab for my Beretta, then replace it in the bottom of my purse. Somehow I know no one is here. They've come, trashed, and left.

The message is loud and clear: We know your routine. Be careful.

It takes me a few minutes to restore my calm and then many more to put the living room back in some sort of order.

Cooking always calms me. Maybe it's the prep, or the first aromas, that do the job; but for some reason, when I'm slicing and cutting, it enables me to think in an orderly manner.

I head to the kitchen. Pull out a medium-sized eggplant, several zucchini, and three juicy tomatoes—the perfect base for a nice ratatouille. I cook two strips of bacon slowly in order to render the drippings, then remove the slices and add olive oil and a couple of minced garlic cloves.

As each vegetable cooks down, the aromas burst forth to fill the space around me. While the ratatouille simmers, I pop a couple of bread slices into the toaster and pour a mug of coffee.

By the time I take my second breakfast onto the deck, I have sifted through what must have happened the night before.

Even though I didn't find evidence of forced entry, someone has easily breeched, entered, and then trashed the living room. Why? There's nothing of any remote value here. What are they looking for?

And then I remember the tiara, which had slipped into the recesses of my mind because of Arlene's untimely death. Someone still must be looking for that tiara. But who?

The suspect list is short. Though their meddling with the law is certainly not above reproach, I can't imagine someone from the other three families invading the privacy of my cottage. As far as I can tell, Fin hasn't shown up. But it would be silly to discount him.

Footsteps on the stone stairs pull me away from my thoughts as Frederick Ashton appears.

"Am I disturbing you, my dear?"

I rise to greet him by waving my mug. "Not at all. Care for some coffee? I was just going to pour myself another mug."

"Oh, my, no thank you. I've already had more than my daily quota."

He follows me through the sliding glass door into the kitchen and takes a deep breath. "Ahh, is that ratatouille I smell?"

I nod, give it a stir, put a lid on it and turn off the fire.

"Care to join me? I have enough for two."

"Oh, thank you, but I'm honor bound to eat only Cook's fare. Don't want to be disloyal."

Ashton waits while I pour my coffee, and then follows me into the living room.

Once I'm on the couch, he settles in the chair next to me and says, "Teenie Herold stopped by to tell me the news about Arlene. I'm so sorry."

"Thank you for your concern. Arlene's funeral was very sad. The church only half full."

Ashton looks down for a few seconds, then says, "At least Sallie and Arlene will be together now. I guess that's some sort of consolation."

He stares at the ceiling for a few seconds, then looks slowly about the room until he spots the commode with the door hanging askew. "Goodness me, what happened here?"

I see the raised eyebrows and the question in his eyes, and for some reason it dawns that maybe Frederick Ashton's name should be added to my short list of suspects. There's no doubt in my mind that Aunt Sallie and he were close. Maybe she had told him about the tiara.

I give him an innocent shrug. "I found it that way when I returned to the compound this morning. There were cocktail napkins and bar tools scattered all over the floor.

"Thing is, I'm positive the cottage was secure when I left last night. But this isn't the first time there's been evidence that someone ... someone with a key ... has dropped by to make their presence known."

He flashes me a brief smile. "Maybe it was a raccoon or some sort of animal."

I shake my head. "If it was a raccoon, it would have to be one damn smart varmint."

Ashton nods, then turns to study the commode for a moment. "That door shouldn't be too difficult to repair. But you might have to take the whole piece to Utica." Then he murmurs, "Must have been something at one time, though when I first saw it, the marble top was already badly stained."

He turns to face me. "I take it you're back for a while?"

"Looks that way."

"Any plans for house guests that I should know about?" When I don't respond right away, Ashton hurries on.

"Please don't think I'm being nosy. It's just that several members of the families have inquired about you and are wondering when you will be joining us in the boathouse for dinner."

Big fat lie! Anyone who asks about me is just an overly curious acquaintance who is upset that I have inherited the cottage and have refused to sell it. But it's obvious that the current gossip is that I'm continuing to investigate Sallie's murder. A murder the families are trying so hard to believe was a suicide.

Ashton clears his throat several times before I finally say, "Don't worry, I'll give you plenty of notice before I descend on the boathouse."

"The last few days have been pretty rough. You know, finding Arlene so close by, then dealing with the sad reality of her death. Worse still, poor Uncle Aiden suffered a mild stroke when he first heard the news, though his doctor assured me that he'll fully recover."

Ashton stands. "I'm glad to hear that." The words are solicitous but the tone in his voice gives the impression that he never gave a damn about Uncle Aiden.

He turns toward the sliding glass door before saying, "Well, now that I've seen that you're safely in, I'll be on my way."

When I call out, "Thanks so much for checking on me," he pauses and turns. "By the way, my dear, there's supposed to be a front coming through later this morning."

"Really? I haven't been paying much attention to the weather. No TV and the radio fades in and out depending on the traffic on 28. Thanks for the heads-up."

He gives me a smart salute. "Just doing my job. If you need anything, please feel free to call me. Any time."

CHAPTER 34

It's just past noon when the first blustery squall line, followed by heavy rain, comes through. Not that I didn't believe Ashton's warning, but in my preoccupation with the missing tiara, I had forgotten all about it.

After racing from room to room shutting the windows, I nuke the last of the coffee and make myself half a peanut butter and jelly sandwich for lunch.

Ashton may or may not have been in my cottage last night, but his latest visit has prompted me to climb to the second floor and open the upstairs hall closet to get the old boathook that was used to pull down the attic stairs.

If someone is in fact looking for that tiara, I'm going to have to find it before they do.

How many times had Arlene and I watched Aunt Sallie lift the boathook to the ceiling and pull? Then we would clamber upwards and she would follow.

Now, even after all these years, I still feel the familiar creaks and groans of the rickety contraption beneath my steps.

In the attic gloom I barely make out the light bulb hanging from the center rafter. This will be my first time to turn it on. Arlene and I were too small to reach that high back then.

Over the years we both grew taller, but by the time we were able to reach the light, we were no longer fighting over the tiara, or playing dress-up. We had discovered boys.

I cross the creaking floorboards to the trunk in the far corner. It's not as large as I remember, but then it's been over twenty years since Arlene and I were up here.

I settle beside the trunk, lift the lid, and smile. The several pairs of sparkly heels are still there. Once they seemed gigantic, but now they wouldn't fit my foot even if I could lop off a few toes.

Next are the tangled strands of fake pearls. Still intact. I negotiate one strand carefully out of the mass, hang it around my neck, and place the pile on the floor.

I slowly lift out the first feather boa and then the second. Considering their advanced age, they're pretty much as I remember except for the fifty-odd loose feathers that float back into the now-bare bottom of the trunk.

No tiara. Fake or not, it's either already been heisted or it's still safely tucked away in an undiscovered hiding place.

Fin didn't find it. And if it was Frederick Ashton who was snooping around last night, he obviously came up empty-handed as well.

I carefully return all the items to the trunk and lower the lid on the past. Then let the tears that have been cramming the backs of my eyes ever since I discovered Arlene's body trickle down my cheeks.

I didn't cry when I found Arlene. I didn't cry when they body-bagged her and drove her through the Hotanawa gates, and I could not shed one tear during her funeral. I was too angry. My best buddy had betrayed me. Overdosed on meth. Killed herself and maybe left an untended infant behind.

Above, the rain pounds against the metal roof, drowning out my sobs. I lower my head to rest against the lid of the trunk and remember the happy times Arlene and I spent playing pretend, and fighting over who would be princess first and get to wear that fake tiara.

The storm has passed by the time I shove the stairs upward and close the attic entry. Next step is to stow the boathook back in the linen closet. That done, I start to shut the closet door, then pull it wide.

I had never paid much attention to that closet as a child except when I scrambled from my icy cold bed to search for an extra blanket.

Now that I study it, I realize the closet is deeper than most. The newly arrived but unopened packages of twin sheets, pillowcases, and several cotton blankets are stacked neatly on the three lower shelves. Above and out of my reach is the upper shelf, lined with old Crane & Co. stationery boxes labeled: BUTTONS, THREAD, MISC. PATCHES, SEWING KIT, and one box that has no label.

I think back to the tiara Arlene and I had fought over. Could it possibly fit in that unlabeled box? Wouldn't that be the perfect hiding place? Right there in plain sight?

It's then I remember that there used to be an upstairs step stool and turn to the closet directly across from the linens. I open that door and *voilá*.

That closet was Uncle Aiden's. Besides being home for the step stool, it houses plastic boxes filled with battery-powered tools, nails, screws; a stack of instructions for said power tools; as well as several assorted handsaws.

After placing the stool next to the shelves, I climb up the four steps but hesitate to step on the fifth. Balance has never been one of my strong points, and even though it's not to my advantage, I feel much safer on the step below.

Even then, my perilous foothold makes my upward reach unsteady. Hand trembling, I manage to inch the box towards me with my fingertips. Finally, gravity wins. The unwieldy box hurtles past, out of my reach, and I watch helplessly as it hits the floor.

The lid pops off.

Empty.

No. Not quite empty: A small, old-fashioned key lies on the wood floor next to the lid.

I stand there on the step stool, clinging to the top shelf, staring down at the key, wondering if I'll be able to get safely down without falling.

Once safely on solid ground, I pick up the key and shove it in my jeans pocket; then place the lid on the empty box and stash it in the tool closet, along with the step stool.

CHAPTER 35

The temperature has dropped at least twenty degrees. On Fourth Lake, whitecaps have formed, rocking the pontoon party boats like bathtub toys. It may be July, but today, Mother Nature has chosen to ignore that fact.

I grab a fleece jacket from the row of pegs on the workshop wall, turn on the oven, and set a fire in the living room. In a very short time, Holden Cottage is as cozy as it can be under the circumstances.

After pouring the last of the single malt in my glass, I settle on the couch before the fire and then inch the key from my pocket.

It's a quaint key from a bygone era, its head a lovely filigreed triangle. The kind of key you wiggle into a keyhole and move it around until it clicks in place. But this key is small—too small for the door to the commode that holds the liquor.

I've seen that key before. But where? In this cottage, of course. But what does it open? Why can't I remember?

When I lean forward to place the key on the coffee table before me, my stomach growls, and I realize the half of the peanut butter sandwich I hastily crammed down my craw at noon is long gone, and I'm starving.

It's just past six when I retrieve a seasoned chicken breast from the fridge and throw it into a small skillet.

While the ratatouille simmers and the chicken browns, I crack open a nice Sauvignon Blanc, and in minutes I'm settled back in front of the fire, digging in.

That's when the pounding begins, accompanied by a woman's angry, "I know you're in there, you sonovabitch. Open up! Now!"

Realizing that sounds travel quickly along the lakeshore, I hurry to open the door.

I'm not prepared for the skinny blonde who strides past me into the living room.

"Where the hell is he?"

I shut the door behind me. "Who?"

"Witcher, that's who."

My heart drops into my stomach.

"Who wants to know?"

The blonde points to a large gold circle on the ring finger of her left hand. "His wife."

My brain scrambles. Wife? I flash back to the whispered conversation Liam had the first night we spent together. Was that his wife calling? The thought makes me feel ill.

The attorney in me takes charge. Liam never said he had been married. Not that that means anything these days. But I really haven't done anything terribly wrong according to the mores of the moment, so I have little reason to feel guilty.

I point the blonde to the chair next to the couch. "Have a seat. Would you like some wine or maybe something a little stronger?"

She ignores me and heads for the kitchen. "Hey, Witcher! I'm runnin' out of patience, you better get your ass in here!"

I've heard that voice before, but where? When? I throw those thoughts aside to hurry behind her. "I told you Witcher isn't here. What did you say your name was?"

"I didn't, but I know who you are, you sleazy slut."

I resist the temptation to grab her arm and yank her back into the living room.

Instead, I use a soothing tone. "I can understand why you're upset. But I'm telling you, this is all one big mistake. Why don't we take a seat by the fire and have a little chat?"

At those words, tears replace her bluster. She follows me to the living room and collapses into the chair next to the hearth.

I edge between the coffee table and the hearth to reach the commode. I pour some of Uncle Aiden's single malt into a glass, hand it to her, then settle on the hearth next to her chair.

After she downs the drink, she hugs her arms around her body and begins to rock back and forth. That's when I first notice the ragged fingernails and the gnawed cuticles.

And that gets my attention. Hair sort of straggly, jeans patchy, but not because they're in the three-hundred-dollar-a-pair range. And under a shapeless cardigan, her T-shirt is spotted with stains.

I am so dense! This woman is sky high on meth. I tick through the symptoms: nervous twitches, teeth jagged and discolored, and her eyes ... I shudder, remembering the same dead look in Arlene's eyes.

"Okay now, how about a name?"

She tries to focus. "Uh-uh-*what?*"

"Your name?"

"It's Bren—Brenda Witcher."

Could she be the same Brenda who was at Fin's house the day I sent Liam's raid south? Is that why Liam is a narcotics investigator? Because his wife is hooked?

I shake my head in disbelief. Does that mean Liam is a double-crosser?

The irony of that statement isn't lost on me. Liam may be double-crossing me in more ways than one.

"And you're Liam Witcher's wife?" I ask, not wanting to hear the answer.

"Uh, n-no. My husband is his brother."

I practically collapse with relief until the stone at the bottom of my stomach begins to grow. I don't recall Liam ever talking about a brother, and the skinny blonde still hasn't given me her husband's name. Suddenly the whole thing reads fishy.

"You say that Liam's brother has left you?"

"Yeah. He's gone."

"And why do you think he's here?"

Her eyes dart back and forth several times before she murmurs, "I overheard something at the Big M."

Ah. The Big M. How many false scenarios have taken root at the Big M?

"So. You overheard something at the grocery store?"

Eyes still darting, she gives me a questioning look, then says, "Yes, I did. It was Artie Curtis. I'd know his voice anywhere."

She seems to be waiting for some sort of reaction from me and when I give none, she stammers, "Y-you k-know Artie Curtis, don't you?"

When I nod, she smiles and then says, "Well, ya see, Artie was telling one of the other men who works up here at the compound that my W-Witcher's been spending nights at Holden Cottage."

Brenda lets out a shuddering sigh, then sees my smile, and blurts out, "Hey, this isn't supposed to be funny."

"It is when you've got the wrong guy. I have been seeing a *Liam* Witcher, but not up here."

Her reaction to my statement is a shocker because she jumps up, throws her arms in a strangle hold around my neck, and squeals, "Liam? And not my baby? Oooh, that changes everything."

Something is definitely not right. Only minutes ago this woman barged in shouting obscenities, and now she's cooing like a dove.

She steps away, lowers her eyes, and mumbles, "I'm so sorry about all this. Really, I am. It was a big mistake."

I watch as she takes a couple steps backward and then hurries toward the front door, opens it, and waves a timid goodbye.

I stand there, mouth agape with incredulity. What just happened? Ten minutes ago a woman called Brenda stormed into the cottage, slinging accusations, and then just as suddenly, cooed her goodbyes and disappeared.

I'm still processing the event as I pick up my plate and take it into the kitchen to nuke it.

Once I'm re-settled in front of the fire, I take a few sips of the

Sauvignon Blanc and then dig in to my rudely delayed supper as I go over the day's events.

Could Ashton and Brenda's visits somehow be connected? Doesn't seem possible since I'm almost positive that the voice I heard at Fin's was hers.

But yet, even though Frederic Ashton has been Hotanawa's trusted retainer for years, I haven't felt right about the man since he first showed me the letter from Aunt Sallie.

I carry the dishes into the kitchen and, after stacking them in the sink, I fish beneath the phone book and Aunt Sallie's notebook to retrieve the heavy, cream-colored envelope from the bottom of the drawer.

I check the postmark. Just as I thought, the envelope had been stamped the day Aunt Sallie was murdered. The tone of the letter to "Freddy" is exactly as I recall. But after the re-read, I feel even more convinced that Sallie and Ashton were having an affair—an affair that had lasted for years. And if that were so, my take is that Sallie had probably told him about the tiara.

I put the envelope back in its hiding place, and return to the sink and my final chore of the day. The last dish is in the drainer when I remember the key.

On first search, I come up empty-handed. The coffee table in front of the hearth is bare, as is the floor beneath it, and the floor beneath the couch.

And then I recall the movement behind me while I was preparing the drink for Brenda. That had to be when she snatched it.

Damn it! That bitch was sent with only one mission—to get that key. The whole story was a ruse to get in my house and steal the only concrete clue right from under my nose. But who sent her? My first hunch is Fin, but still, it could be Frederick Ashton.

CHAPTER 36

The following morning I chugalug my coffee and cram Woods' finest pastry down my craw.

While tossing and turning my way through the long night, I have made a plan.

Despite Liam's repeated warnings about returning to the caretaker's cabin, I park next to the cottage, arm myself, and head up the rutted road.

I judge it's a half-mile from Holden Cottage to the large, moss-covered glacial erratic boulder common to the Adirondacks and then some twenty yards more to the abandoned cabin.

The front door, slightly ajar, swings wide at my touch. The heavy odor of recently cooked meth hangs in the air, but the kitchen is bare. I check the stove for heat. Stone cold.

Nothing else seems to have changed except for a wide swath trailing through the dust and debris on the living room floor, leading to the half-open bedroom door. Could be from a large bag filled with something heavy or ... I shiver at the thought that it might be from a body.

Inside the right pocket of my fleece, my hand clutches the grip of the Beretta, safety off, ready to draw, as I take the ten or so steps to the door, and push it open with my shoe.

On the bed, facing the wall, hands cuffed behind her back, and wearing the same outfit she had on the night before, lies Brenda, the scraggly blonde who heisted my key.

– 158 –

I peek to the right through the door crack. Nothing. Then, with my weapon engaged, I swing left through the opening and into the room.

Satisfied that it's empty except for the woman, I pocket my Beretta and start for the bed.

I lean over, check her carotid, and find a thready pulse.

That's when the door to the bath flies open and two men in ski masks leap into the room.

One of them steps behind me as the other motions to my right pocket. "Hand it over."

I look into Fin's bright blue eyes, relax a little, and give him a slight smile. Somewhere under there is the boy who kissed me that summer, fifteen years ago. If I can just remind him of the way things used to be ...

His only response is to raise his weapon. "Now! Or you're dead."

"Okay, okay. Don't get your nose in a knot." I take a step toward him to surrender my Beretta into his outstretched hand, then stop when Fin pulls his weapon off me.

He's looking behind me. "What in hell? You?"

Figuring I'm no longer in his line of fire, I drop to one knee, Beretta at the ready.

I'm about to check the noise behind me when excruciating pain fills the back of my head and my world goes black.

⌒⤬⌒

Liam's voice travels through the fog in my brain. "It's about time you came to. Looks like somebody gave you quite a whack on the head."

I mumble, "Where am I? How long have I been here?"

"You're in your room at Woods, courtesy of the local police. They brought you here yesterday, after a doc in Old Forge checked you over and pronounced there was no evidence of a concussion. I came as soon as I could."

I fade out again, but Liam's next words pull me back to reality. "Hey. Try to focus here for a minute, okay? I didn't get much sleep last night and they want answers."

I struggle my eyelids to half-mast and watch Liam reach into his jacket pocket and pull out an envelope. "You kept muttering about some key. I sure hope this is it."

He rips open the envelope and the old-fashioned key with the filigreed head drops into his hand.

"Thank heaven! How did you get this?"

"Don't ask."

"I'll need that as soon as I wake up."

He pockets the key, then helps me to a sitting position.

When a wave of nausea surges, I squint, then shut my eyes, and murmur, "Hey, there, I'm a little off my land-legs. Let's take a little nap first, okay?"

"Nuh-uh. We can't wait any longer. The state police and forensics were at the cabin. They swept the place and removed the body, and just a few minutes ago Chief Zandt gave me the bad news."

"What body?"

I don't like the look in Liam's eyes, or the tone of his voice. And I really don't like his next words.

"I think they said she was Brenda. Does that ring a bell? Forensics alleges that the four bullets in the back of that woman on the bed were fired from your Beretta."

"But I never fired my weapon. You have to believe me."

"Sorry, but the lands and grooves on the bullets they removed from her body match those test-fired from your Beretta. And worse still, only your prints were found on the weapon."

That gets my attention. I'm wide-awake. I gasp, mind racing through those last moments in the caretaker's cabin: Brenda facing away from me; the two men in ski masks—one that I'm dead positive was Fin Holden.

Then the others came in. I remember dropping to one knee to aim my weapon, but that was as far as I got. There was a blow to my head and the lights went out.

"No, no, no. That's not at all what happened. I saw her on the bed, checked for a carotid pulse just before the two masked men appeared out of the loo. I swear to you, that woman—Brenda—was alive. And then someone cold-cocked me from behind. Hey, wait a minute. How can they run a lands and grooves test so fast?"

Liam gives me that crooked smile. "It's been twenty-four hours, Allie. Plenty of time to run the test a couple of times."

I feel an ache in my right hand and hold it up for Liam to see. "See these bruises? I got them because someone put my weapon in my hand and held it in place, then squeezed the trigger."

Liam pulls his Walther from its holster, wraps my hand around the grip, then covers it with his. "I guess that's possible. But it's a really tight squeeze in the trigger department."

"Maybe that's the reason for the four shots." I let out a long sigh. "I hate to tell you this, but Fin was one of the men."

"You've got to be kidding."

I shake my head. "I wish I were. There was a scuffle behind me and when Fin pulled his aim away from me, I dropped to one knee. That's when I was knocked out.

"There's something else. Something very important, but I can't remember exactly what."

I let out a long sigh. No point in dragging something up that may or may not be relevant.

CHAPTER 37

I've been holed up at The Woods Inn for a couple of days. Sad to say, I remain the major suspect in Brenda's (or whatever-her-real-name-is) murder.

There is one bright spot in my black world. It seems that some hikers had wandered across the highway from the trailhead parking area, saw the cabin with the door wide open, and walked in.

When they got to the bedroom, they discovered me in a pool of blood on the floor, and Brenda dead.

Even though forensics said there were no fingerprints that could be identified other than mine, the case against me is not as strong as it seemed in the beginning, thanks to those kids who found me unconscious.

Chief Zandt has assigned a local uniform, who worked with Liam on a couple of joint drug operations, to be my point man. Bottom line: The guy is here to keep an eye on me.

But I have news for Zandt. He may think he's in charge, but I can do more in an unofficial capacity than he or his point man can. That's been proven loud and clear.

But maybe now they finally believe me—that we're not dealing with suicide here. We're dealing with cold-blooded murder. And I don't care what Clarissa Napier and the "Natawas" have offered him—he can't ignore the truth any longer.

As my bruises matured, Liam agreed with my theory about how my fingerprints got on the butt of my Beretta. And then "Brenda's" (last name unknown) autopsy report revealed she was laced with drugs and, most probably, near dead when she was shot.

The bruises on my right hand, and a quick demo by Liam and me to illustrate how such bruising could have occurred, prompted Chief Zandt to agree that I probably had been set up, but even though I have my point man, he's warned me not to leave the area.

Liam has been a huge help, and is really shaping up to be someone I can depend on. I feel a little guilty that I ever doubted him.

The pain from the whack has greatly subsided, but each time I look in a mirror I can't ignore the fact that I just barely missed meeting my maker.

∽⁀

My return to Holden Cottage following the incident at the caretaker's cabin is uneventful. No bells and whistles, just Liam's unmarked car turning in on the exit road, passing the scene of "my" crime, and finally stopping at the cottage.

During my brief absence, Hotanawa has taken on new life. Kids are squealing, tennis balls are thwacking against opposing rackets, and, at the dock below, Sunfish sails flap in the breeze.

I step inside the living room to see vases of ferns and daisies set on the coffee table and the lopsided commode. "Did you do this?"

"No way. Looks like Ashton's been hard at work. He was so concerned when he heard what happened, that he's called my cell every day to check on you. Hope you don't mind."

"Oh, Liam, how could I ever have suspected Ashton? He's been nothing but kindness itself."

He pulls me into his arms. "I don't think he was ever very high on your list of suspects, was he?"

As I let Liam kiss me, I think to myself that there are *two* people whom I seriously misjudged. But he doesn't need to know about the other.

∽∾

The afternoon is warm and the promise of a balmy evening sends Liam into Inlet for take-out pizza, which we share along with a nice bottle of Chianti at the table on the deck overlooking the lake.

The days are shortening little by little, but at seven o'clock the sun hangs high enough to warm the kids still in the water.

A wave of nostalgia rolls over me at the familiar sounds, echoing those of my childhood.

Though the tragic deaths of Aunt Sallie and Arlene will remain with me forever, those sounds from my past will always be a comforting contrast.

Liam breaks through my reveries. "Guess we better head back to Woods before it gets too dark. I've got to run to Albany for a meeting tomorrow."

"Some kinda fair-weather friend you are. The minute I'm feeling a little perky, off you go." I smile when I say it, but I really sort of mean it.

His smile fades. "You know I wouldn't move an inch from your side if it wasn't necessary."

I lean up to kiss his cheek. "I'm kidding. Where's your sense of humor?"

"I guess I lost it at the caretaker's cabin. What if those kids hadn't come by when they did? What if the police had found you and that woman both dead? And because the Beretta clutched in your hand matched the bullets in her body, you would have been branded a criminal. This is serious, Allie. Somebody has set you up. They want you gone."

I look away to hide beginning tears. I can't let Liam see how frightened I really am. I don't want his pity. I got myself into this mess because I couldn't control my curiosity. And because I couldn't, I made a stupid mistake that almost cost me my life.

I try to change the subject, or at least turn it away from my problem. "I'm sure Fin was counting on my curiosity to draw me to the cabin. I'm positive he sent that woman."

Liam shakes his head. "Don't make light of this, Allie. I think a lot more is going on than we know. Much more."

❧

It's dark when insistent knocking wakes me. "Allie, it's me. Let me in. Something really important has happened."

I hear the urgency in Liam's voice, turn on the lamp, and check the time. It's almost eleven.

When I open the door, he throws his arms around me. "I was so afraid I wouldn't make it back before ..."

I see the fear in his eyes and my heart begins to pound in tune with each word I hear. "They found Fin at the south end of Twin Pond. He and his sidekick were killed execution-style.

"They're running tests but forensics says they were killed the day they were at the cabin." He pauses, then murmurs, "Both were shot in the back of the head. They've been in the water ever since."

With each word, my heartbeat ratchets up a notch as the stone in my stomach grows.

"You know what this means, don't you?" I manage to say, my voice emerging as a croak.

"Yeah, we have a major problem to face. The police are pretty sure the people who killed Fin and his accomplice have us on their hit list. That's why I broke every speed law coming up from Alder Creek."

I try to absorb everything Liam has just said. But first time through it makes no sense. "Why would these people waste time on us?"

Liam slumps and lets out a long sigh. "I think they want me out of the way. And you're my Achilles heel."

CHAPTER 38

It's Thursday and Teenie has arrived. As soon as Teenie has her instructions, Liam and I head for Old Forge. We're finally, the both of us, taking a much-needed day off. I don't want to think about murders and executions and drownings. I just want to get my hair done.

After a cut and blow dry, I meet Liam at the triangle in front of Old Forge Hardware, where he looks me over and gives me an approving smile.

We finally agree on lunch at nearby Five Corners Café to share a quiche and a bottle of wine under an umbrella on the side patio.

After Liam pays the check, he suggests we return to Inlet via the South Shore Road so we can pick up some meat for supper.

At the thought of passing Twin Pond, where Fin's body had been found, a shiver courses through me.

Fin's last words replay: *"What in hell? You?"*

Why didn't I remember what he said? I'm about to tell Liam, when he rises and starts for the parking lot, leaving me to chase behind.

I catch up and put my hand on his arm to stop him. And then I say, "I just remembered something really important."

"What?"

"I—I'm pretty sure Fin knew whoever was standing behind me."

Liam grabs my hand and pulls me along until we reach the car.

After we settle in our seats and shut both doors, he turns to me. "Repeat what you just said."

I do, then say, "After Fin took charge of the situation, I remember his partner stepping behind me. But then I heard another person—or maybe two more people—come into the bedroom, and then Fin says, *'What in hell? You?'*"

Liam's really pissed because his voice is low and his words evenly spaced. "You never said one word about hearing other people."

I shrug and give him a lame, "I'm so sorry, but it just came to me now."

He shakes his head and clenches his jaws a few times. "This is a pretty significant piece of evidence that you conveniently forgot to remember."

"I must have been suppressing."

But why is Liam so angry?

My flimsy excuse hangs in the air as Liam starts the car, heads past the Catholic Church to turn left toward the Old Forge Pond, and then veers right past the Town of Webb Professional Offices and up South Shore Road.

He drives the next few miles in silence, while I stare straight ahead, trying to figure out a proper explanation for why I had experienced such a total lapse of memory. Did I want to forget those last seconds? Did I want to forget Fin's words?

And those words? Why did I block them out?

Liam's ringing cell breaks into my thoughts.

He pulls to the side of the road to answer, then nods his head as he says, "Look, I told you this morning there would be no problem and I meant it." He listens but shakes his head at every word he hears. "Okay, okay, if you think it's really necessary, come ahead. I'm already parked."

A few seconds later he turns to peer out the back window. "Okay, now I see you."

Liam puts his cell on the console and gives me a brief smile. "I have some unfinished business from a meeting I had this morning while you were getting your hair done. Not to worry. Stay put. This won't take long."

When the car pulls in behind us, Liam steps out to meet the emerging uniform.

I don't pay too much attention since the man looks vaguely familiar.

Then I yawn and smile to myself. As I had hoped, the two glasses of wine at lunch have made me drowsy. I lean back against the head-rest, relax, and nod off.

I have no idea how much time has passed before I hear Liam yelling my name.

What happens next happens so quickly that I barely have time to turn around.

Liam is face down and pinned against the hood of the car, and the uniform is cuffing him. Then the man drags him to the rear door and shoves him into the back seat.

Before I can move, the car makes a U-turn and speeds away towards Old Forge.

It takes me a few seconds to gather my wits. I open the door, but when I try to stand, I'm shaking so violently, I'm forced to wait until my strength returns.

After I stumble around the car and climb in the driver's side, I realize Liam has left his cell behind.

I press the "recents" symbol and a list pops onto the screen. All the calls read, "blocked number" with "unknown" beneath.

I roll through the telephone numbers to "Webb Police" and press it.

"This is Chief Zandt. How may I help you?"

"This is Allie Armington, Chief Zandt."

"Oh? Oh, yes."

Every minute counts, so I cut to the chase. "I wonder if you could please tell me why one of your men has arrested Liam Witcher?"

The silence on the other end is deafening. Then Zandt says, "I didn't issue such an order. And why would I arrest one of my own?"

"But I'm an eyewitness. Detective Witcher and I were driving on the South Shore Road toward Inlet when he got a call on his cell. We pulled to the side of the road so he could take the call and, shortly after that, a patrol car pulled up behind us."

I quickly relate the incident, ending with, "All this happened not more than five minutes ago."

Again the dead silence, then Chief Zandt says, "Well, I'm looking out the window at our patrol cars and not one is missing."

He must hear my gasp, because he offers, "Would it be too difficult for you to come by the office for a few minutes to give me the details again? The Webb Police stands ready to help you in any way we can."

Well, that's a first. If anything is going to wake the Webb Police up, it's going to be a loss of one of their own.

⊱✶⊰

The drive into Old Forge seems to take forever. Though I've never been to the Town of Webb Police station, I vaguely remember that it's located across Route 28 from the Visitor Information Center.

The problem with turning left on the highway during the tourist season is finding a break in the oncoming traffic. Even though it's not the weekend, it is August, and the traffic is already bumper-to-bumper.

Finally, someone takes pity on me—and the impatient line of cars building behind me—and stops so I can get across the lane into the parking lot.

Chief Zandt's face is filled with sympathy. He waves a young officer to join us and asks me to follow him into his office.

"This officer will be taking down the information so we can start the ball rolling as soon as possible. When it's one of ours, time is of the essence.

"While you were driving in, I did a little checking. As I told you when we talked, none of our patrol cars were out. But I thought it would be a good idea to call Inlet. Seems they had a couple cars out on patrol."

I brighten at that. "I didn't think about the Inlet Police—maybe that's who came after Liam. But I still can't figure why the officer would treat him that way."

Zandt shrugs. "You got me there. Thing is, the guys from Inlet only patrol Hamilton County, not Herkimer." He pauses, then says, "Could you make out what it said on the side of the car?"

I shut my eyes, trying to remember. "The car was white. The lettering was dark—navy or black. Could it have been a television news car? I keep visualizing the CBS logo."

Zandt shakes his head. "I think I would have heard if national television was in the area. The stations in Syracuse and Utica are pretty good about letting us know in advance."

Sure they are, I think. And the Tanawas are good at making sure the media has no reason to be in the area.

I sigh. "I've been trained to observe details. It's part of my job, but I was so concerned about Liam, I wasn't ..."

"That's understandable."

He rises. "The good news is there's not much going on around here, so there's no reason we can't mount a full search immediately."

I'm thankful for his help, but it hurts a little when I remember how quick the same man was to rule my Aunt Sallie's death as a suicide and let the person who killed her roam free.

Zandt motions for the officer to leave and then accompanies me to the front door. Once there, he lays a restraining hand on my arm and murmurs, "I don't know if you know, but Liam told me about this current situation this morning. Best you go back to Woods right away, but keep in touch."

"Thanks," I say, and walk back out to my car.

On the drive up Route 28 to The Woods Inn, I can't help but wonder exactly what the "current situation" is. I replay the strange way Liam was taken. Who was it that called him just a few minutes beforehand? Was it the person who took him? Was it someone Liam trusted who turned bad?

Or was the whole thing a setup for my benefit? A way to get Liam out of the crossfire, just moments after I revealed a crucial clue?

The thought of it sends terrifying shivers down my spine.

Is the whole town corrupt? And have I been cavorting with a murderer?

CHAPTER 39

It's three a.m. when I sit bolt upright, shoved out of my sleep as if someone has physically pushed me.

As Liam's capture replays frame by frame, my T-shirt, heavy with sweat, clings to my body.

The hotel is silent. Through the open window all I hear is the rhythmical slap of lake against shore and leaves rustling in the pre-dawn breeze.

I pore over every moment of the past day, remembering how happy I had been at lunch until Liam mentioned going back to Hotanawa via the South Shore Road past Twin Pond.

It was then I remembered what Fin had said. It was then, when I told Liam, that everything started to go to hell.

I take a couple of deep breaths and concentrate on the other car. There was writing on the front door, but what? Think! What did I see? Was it the CBS logo? A stylized eye?

My heart ratchets up a notch as I visualize the eye of a predatory bird. And beneath it the two words: "Falcon Security."

Even though it's still dark, I take a quick shower to clear my head, letting the water cascade down my body until the heat turns tepid.

Fully awake, I pull on a clean tee and khakis, and climb on the Internet.

There are several listings for Falcon Security. One in New Jersey piques my immediate interest. The usual boilerplate fills the first page, but at the end of the hype is a caveat in fine print: This offshore corporation is privately held.

It doesn't really matter. The logo at the top of the site is the same as the one on the side of the car. After spending the next hour trying to get farther into the site without any results, I give up and curl up on the bed fully clothed.

My cell's insistent ring pulls me into mid-morning. It's Chief Zandt. "Nothing on this end. Anything on yours?" It seems the chief is all of a sudden working for the good guys. Or maybe he's just trying to make up for his former sins.

"Not a peep. But I remember the name on the side of that car. Ever heard of Falcon Security?"

"Can't say that I have, but we'll get on that right away."

I want to tell him that I've gone as far as I can go, but the ball is in his court and there may be a few tricks they have up their sleeves that I don't. At this point, it's the least they could do.

Zandt lets out a long breath, then pronounces, "Sad to say, Miss Armington, Detective Witcher is now listed as officially missing."

⌒×⌒

It's almost noon when I hear the familiar "ding" signaling an incoming text. The message is brief. "Twenty-four hours to produce the tiara. Don't waste your time tracing us. We're watching you."

I read the words a second time, heart racing at mach speed. Who are these people? Why do they think I can produce the diamond tiara?

And just how can they be watching me?

Worse still, if I can't find the blasted thing in time, Liam is dead.

Of course there's still one possibility that's worse: Liam is the one who's texting.

I immediately call Chief Zandt with the news. At least I might have an ally of some sort. "What now?"

He doesn't hesitate. "We'll keep on it here. You better keep on looking there."

❧

I place a frustrating call to Ardythe, who denies knowing any-thing about any tiara. She says, "Please don't call Dad about this. He's barely got his pins under him, though I must say, Myra Stetson's atten-tions have been the perfect tonic."

For the first time since Liam was taken, a warmth floods through me and, for a few seconds, I forget my own troubles.

"Oh, Ardythe, that's such good news. Give him a big hug for me."

We chat for a few more minutes and then the conversation ends. Though I'm thrilled that Uncle Aiden is on the mend at last, I realize I've wasted valuable time.

❧

After opening the windows in the cottage living room, I settle at the kitchen table, and pull the key from my pocket to examine it for the umpteenth time.

Too small for a door to a room. Too big for a diary. Could be for a cabinet or a drawer.

I spend the next hour checking every piece of furniture throughout the cottage for small keyholes. Not one.

Then I case the bookshelves in the living room, carefully pulling out and replacing each volume in its rightful slot.

The two upstairs storage closets are next. Defying my fear of heights, I climb the ladder to the top step and cling to the middle shelf as I use a yardstick to probe the depths of the top, dodging what-ever falls past me to the floor. That done, I open every box and paw through every container. Nothing.

I abandon the mess until Teenie's next visit, return to the kitchen, and go online to type: "tiara."

No surprises there. Tiaras come in all sizes and shapes. There's even a Tiara fishing boat. Never heard of that. What am I missing? Two hours since the text. Twenty-two left.

And then I realize I'm starving, and grab a Snickers Bar from the box in the pantry.

Three bars later, and high on sugar, I start a pot of coffee. The high won't last long, and I'll need to stay awake for at least one more swipe through the cottage before I head back to Woods for the evening.

I've just taken my first sip of the tangy, steaming liquid, when there's a tap on the sliding glass door.

My watch reads seven-thirty. Dinner at the boathouse must be in full swing.

When I see who it is, I quickly paste a welcoming smile on my face and let Frederick Ashton in.

He presents me with a mass of delicate ferns wrapped in a soggy paper towel.

"I was delighted to see that you hadn't left for Inlet yet. Do you mind my intruding on your privacy for just a few moments?"

For some reason, a shiver tumbles down my spine. Something isn't right about Ashton's timing.

"Shouldn't you be down at the boathouse running the dinner hour?"

He grins. "Caught me! I'm playing hooky tonight. Giving Artie a go at it. It's his first time to take on that job, and because all the families are in Hotanawa for this weekend, he's nervous as a whore in church."

I can't help but laugh. "Wish I were a fly on the wall to see that! Pardon me for saying so, but Artie just doesn't have your *savoir faire*."

I set the steaming mug on the kitchen table and take the ferns.

"I just made a fresh pot of coffee. Care to join me?"

He looks at his watch, then smiles. "That will probably keep me up until the wee hours, but yes, thank you."

I motion Ashton toward the living room. "Have a seat. It'll take just a second to put these in water."

Ashton, seated on the chair next to the fireplace, rises to take the proffered mug.

I place my mug on the coffee table, settle into the cushions on the couch, and then say, "Thank you so much for the phone calls asking about my health."

He lowers his eyes. "It was the least I could do."

After taking a small sip of the coffee and then clearing his throat several times, Ashton says, "The reason for my impromptu visit this evening is to tell you personally that I will be leaving Hotanawa at the end of the season. I didn't want you to hear the news second hand."

I'm surprised by the tears that spring to my eyes. This summer has been filled with so many sad losses and now this.

Ashton moves to sit next to me on the couch and takes my hand in his. "Oh, my dear, I didn't expect this sort of reaction."

"But you're the glue that has kept this compound together."

His act of kindness unleashes the frustrations and sorrows I've been keeping dammed inside me since Liam was taken, and for the next several minutes, I tell him everything that has happened since I discovered Sallie's body lying at the edge of the lake to the threatening text message about the tiara.

When I finish, for a brief moment the heavy burden I've been carrying eases a little, and I accept Ashton's handkerchief.

"I've turned this place upside down looking for that tiara and haven't found a thing except this key that doesn't seem to open anything."

I pull it from my pocket and put it on the coffee table in front of us.

"Arlene and I used to play dress-up in the attic and there was a tiara we used to fight over, but I'm sure it was paste. I just don't get it. Why would anybody think there's a real tiara hidden in this cottage?"

He's silent for a few seconds, and then says, "The first time I saw the tiara was when I first met your Aunt Sallie in Chicago the year she made her debut. I was escort to one of her dearest friends whose family had known mine for years."

I scramble through the fragments of my Aunt Sallie's past to her tale of her debut. "Was that Georgie?"

He smiles. "Indeed it was. Miss Georgianna Ravenstaal, if you please. The Ravenstaals always came to New Providence for the winter months when the weather in Chicago turned dreary, and those arctic gales roared down

Lake Michigan.

"During the family's annual visit to Nassau the winter prior to her debut, Georgie invited me to be her escort. I was delighted to accept the honor, mainly because through the years she had become like a sister to me. Then too, I had never been to the states.

"I arrived several days before the Christmas Cotillion, slept off the lag, and awoke in time to put on my formals and get Georgie to the first event."

He gives me a dreamy smile. "Georgie, of course was elegant, but it was your aunt that stole my heart the instant I gazed upon her. Something about her eyes, something about her voice . . . and that sparkling tiara. She looked every bit a royal."

Ashton murmurs, "I knew the minute she stepped into my arms, I could never let her go."

I give myself a small pat on the back for picking up on that little tidbit, but Aunt Sallie and Uncle Aiden always seemed so happy together. I can't imagine either one of them with anyone else. Still, Frederick Ashton has all but confessed that he and Aunt Sallie had been lovers for years.

"What happened? Why didn't you . . .?"

My question hangs in the air until Ashton says, "My family's wealth was inherited. Unfortunately, Father knew only how to spend, and to add tragedy to dismay, it turned out that he particularly excelled in making bad investments.

"Father died suddenly on the Christmas Day following the cotillion. Being the only child, I was called home to salvage what I could of the family holdings, but to no avail. I had to sell the estate to pay off the debt and then move Mother to a small but acceptable accommodation on the east end of the island.

"By the time I got Mother settled, Sallie and Aiden had become engaged to be married. My princess had been taken.

"I was heartbroken and told her as much, but Sallie said, while she would always love me, Aiden was her rock. How could a penniless bloke like me compete with a rock? Mind you, I have always liked and admired Aiden Armington, but in my heart, Sallie is ... was mine."

"And that's how you were hired on here?"

He nods. "As luck would have it, Sallie's father and I had shared several nice conversations during the festivities surrounding the cotillion and we became good friends.

"The following summer, when Hotanawa lost its original general manager—who had been with families for almost forty years—Sallie's father, knowing about my predicament, suggested me.

"For my part, the job and its time frame were perfect. Arrive mid-May. Depart mid-October. Five months in heaven only yards away from the woman I adored. And then seven months to apply my efforts to other interests.

"Over time, through making shrewd investments, and a modicum of luck, I've done well enough to buy back my family home in Lyford Cay."

He flashes me his winning smile. "You could say my life is one of extreme contrasts."

"And you don't mind?"

"Not in the least. My position has many advantages. As you must know, my role in the compound is very powerful. No one in Hotanawa makes a move without my blessing. Then too, there was another goal to achieve: my beloved Sallie.

"It took several years for the two of us to finally come together. I was patient. Never pushed. Always the loyal friend—until the year after Arlene was born.

"That's when our magical time began. And those first few years, each time we made love in the cottage, Sallie would wear her tiara."

His smile dies. "That magic lasted until this May."

His eyes glisten until he quickly blinks the telltale evidence away, and says, "As you might guess, that's why I'm leaving."

"Then you know where the tiara is?"

"Of course I do. Although that little key had nothing to do with getting to it, it served its purpose to distract."

He steps to the commode and leans down to press the door. To my surprise, not the door, but an opening at the back of the commode, springs open to reveal the tiara.

He hands it to me. "The tiara belongs to you now."

As I take it from him, my mind is crammed with so many questions that need to be asked.

I want to know everything about the tiara. Who made it? Who wore it? How had it ended up at Holden Cottage?

Then those thoughts are blunted by my cell ringing.

When I turn toward the kitchen, Ashton puts a staying hand on my arm, his eyes beseeching mine. "Must you? There's so much more to tell."

I catch a change in the tone of his voice, and pause. The way he's gripping my arm sets off a warning bell somewhere in the back of my mind. Then, ignoring the cautionary stone growing in my gut, I gently push his hand away.

"I have to answer. It might be news about Liam."

CHAPTER 40

I reach the kitchen and answer on the third ring.

"It's Zandt, are you alone?"

"Not really."

"Is it Ashton?"

That's a jolt.

"Yes."

"Don't say anything. Just listen."

I turn toward the living room to check on my guest, but he's sitting where I left him.

"Falcon Security is owned by Ashton Enterprises, Limited. Based in Nassau. Mean anything?"

At those words, the middle of my body disintegrates as dark spots spire before my eyes. Mind reeling, I grab the kitchen table to keep from collapsing to the floor.

Frederick Ashton has just spent the last fifteen minutes weaving such a compelling tale that, idiot that I am, I have bought every word. I look down at the tiara sparkling on the kitchen table and realize the significance of what has just happened.

If I hadn't answered my cell, I might have made it through the encounter without a scratch. Now, Ashton will have to act.

Panic strikes. I'm trapped in an untenable situation with my thoughts too scattered to make a plan.

Zandt's voice pulls me to the present. "You have to stall."

Stall? He must be crazy. Ashton is on a mission and I've just blown the one slim chance I had to avoid his next move.

I hang up and slide my cell into my right pocket, then grab Liam's cell and cram it into my left.

My Beretta in stashed at the bottom of my purse on the counter next to the stove. When I turn, Ashton is standing in the doorway to the kitchen, pointing a revolver equipped with a silencer at me.

How did he get in the cottage without my seeing his weapon? Then I remember the mass of ferns wrapped in a wad of damp newspapers and how I had hurried to put them in water, giving Ashton plenty of time to stow his weapon until it was needed.

"So sorry, my dear, I've really grown quite fond of you and so hoped to avoid this little scene altogether."

Then he sighs. "But my contact in town called me an hour ago to inform me that the Falcon operation has been blown."

He smiles. "I assume that was Chief Zandt?"

I hardly hear his question. I'm too busy trying to get my arms around what I've just been told.

It's then the grim realization hits me. Frederick Ashton is the big fish Liam mentioned when we first met. He heads the syndicate in charge of the meth labs in this area.

"Fin worked for you?"

He nods. "And very well, thank you. Until you compromised him."

"Me? How did I do that?"

"You followed Arlene."

What a perfect setup. Ashton has been posing as the upstanding and highly respected manager of a private compound while making millions by dealing drugs.

I can't let him see how frightened I am, so I go on the attack. "What was the point in taking Liam?"

Ashton smiles. "I'm surprised you have to ask. Insurance, of course. One must always have a contingency plan. It was easy to draw

Liam into play. All my contact had to do was offer him a little bogus information."

He waves his weapon in the direction of the living room. "We might as well be comfortable while we wait, don't you think?"

When I move past him, I'm tempted to try a tackle. He's stepped backwards to let me by and looks a little off-balance. All it would take would be a quick, hard shove. But then what? He's armed and I'm not.

After I take my place on the couch, he moves to the hearth and settles, weapon still aimed at me. "I must say, my dear girl, once you have the proverbial bone between your teeth, you're like a Jack Russell terrier. I've always admired you for that."

I stare at the man I had trusted implicitly only seconds before while my mind struggles to find some sort of solution. What can I do or say to keep Ashton's attention? What is the most outlandish question I can ask? Statement I can make?

There's only one thing that might get to him—one accusation that he would take the time to defend.

"Why did you kill Aunt Sallie?"

Ashton jerks away as if I've hit him. His eyes fill with pain, and I catch the glint of a tear.

But the joke is on me. His response is even more shocking than I could imagine.

His grief is momentarily replaced with a flash of honest admiration. "How on earth did you know?"

My mind scrambles as I try to overcome the shock of hearing a truth I hadn't remotely anticipated. After all, Freddy and Sallie had been longtime lovers.

"I—I heard Fin say he didn't do it. And Uncle Aiden was in Chicago. Even Arlene was high on my list for a while. And Clarissa. A horrible woman, to be sure, but even she wouldn't be capable of something so awful. I have to confess, I never suspected that Aunt Sallie's lover would ..."

My voice stutters to a halt, but the impact of my accusation has faded. Ashton has managed to pull himself together.

"I can assure you, that wasn't the way things were supposed to go. In fact, Sallie and I had been planning her 'escape' for several years, and when last summer ended, Sallie told me she would be ready this May.

"Of course, I was overjoyed." Then he gives a small shrug. "But, as they say, life is what happens while you're making plans.

"Last fall, despite my objections, Fin began his campaign to obtain the ownership of Holden Cottage through marrying Arlene. As you must know, that poor child had been smitten with the boy since she first laid eyes on him."

I nod, remembering how my cousin and I had been fierce rivals the summer Fin finally kissed me.

Ashton takes a sip, then a second. "This is really quite nice. Now, where was I?"

I almost feel like Scheherazade, except in this case the roles are reversed. Ashton seems to want to talk, and Zandt said stall. How can I miss?

"Fin's campaign for the cottage."

"Ahh, yes. When Brenda called to say someone had blown up the lab in the trailer park, I supposed it was Fin and his lab rats making their first move to sabotage the operation. Poor Fin. Intellectually brilliant, but a shade shy in the planning department."

He takes another swallow, savors it for a few seconds, then says, "I knew Fin wanted to ease me out of what he thought was his territory. Poor sod, he didn't realize I was the kingpin. Too bad he felt his place in my organization was secure. Big mistake. Cost him his life."

"And his partner?" I murmur.

"Yes, that man as well. I understand he had small children. I'm sorry for that."

He shakes his head and takes another sip. "When I arrived early, I decided to lodge in the caretaker's cabin rather than open the boathouse sooner than usual. People become curious when routines change.

"And then the explosion in the trailer park cut our production by a third, which meant Brenda and I needed to spend several nights cooking in order to catch up."

"So, you were already here when Sallie arrived?"

"Yes. But I didn't reveal myself to either Sallie or Arlene. In fact, the evening before she died, I called Sallie from my cell to tell her I would be delayed. That's when she wrote me the letter I gave to you when you came to claim the cottage."

He sighs. "Unfortunately, when Sallie returned from the post office that morning, she came to the caretaker's cottage. Whatever possessed her to do that, I can't even begin to imagine, except it had been our secret rendezvous whenever Aiden and the children were in the compound. Nostalgia, I suppose.

"Sad to say, she found Brenda and me engaged on the cot while the last batch of ice was cooling. It was unfortunate, but I'm only human and Brenda could be extremely entertaining.

"Poor dear, it must have been quite a shock to see us like that. I knew I had to stop her, but there was no time to dress completely, so I went after her in my boxers.

"With Brenda's help, I managed get Sallie down to the cottage without attracting Arlene's attention. Later we found our stealth had been a wasted effort, since Arlene was at Fin's getting another bump.

"So you must see why I couldn't let Sallie live. If only she hadn't come that morning, she and I would have been on our way with no one the wiser. But once she found out about my real 'investment,' there was simply too much at stake.

"Of course, I knew the families could be counted on to sweep everything under the rug. They'd do anything to preserve their sterling reputations. It's ridiculous, really. But with drowning as the cause of death, I gambled that the families would have no trouble convincing the authorities not to continue the investigation. And I was right.

"The act itself wasn't easy. I'm not a monster. It broke my heart when Brenda held her underwater."

His eyes fill again and he wipes the tears away with the back of his free hand.

I can't help the wave of sympathy that washes over me, but that lasts only a second. The bastard killed my Aunt Sallie and he's going to pay.

It wasn't "Fin" that Sallie had tried to write on the grocery list, distraught and frightened for her life. It was "Freddy." Only, she hadn't gotten very far.

Ashton let's out a long sigh, checks his watch, then holds out his empty mug. "Would you mind? My throat is terribly dry."

"The pot is in there." I point toward the kitchen, never dreaming he will let me out of his sight, but for some reason, he seems to think he's in complete control.

He isn't. My Beretta is only a few precious steps away.

When he nods, I leave my mug on the table and rise.

I make the kitchen, grab the Beretta, and stick it beneath my tee into the waistband of my jeans and then grab the pot.

I'm not at all surprised by the calm that descends over me as I return to the living room. I know exactly what I'm going to do because I had plotted a similar scenario several years before.

Ashton smiles as I re-enter, completely unaware that I've gained the advantage. A few more steps and all I have to do is dump the scalding liquid on his lap and bring my Beretta into play.

Two more steps and then the stumble.

He screams when the coffee hits his crotch, his weapon flying out of one hand, his mug falling from the other. "You bitch! You're going to pay for this."

I take a few precautionary steps back, empty pot still clutched in my left hand, weapon aimed.

After a few minutes, he lets his breath slowly out and gives me a pleading look. "Do an old and grieving fellow a favor and take him out. I'm already living in hell."

I pity the poor man. Hate that his life is in shreds. But he killed my Aunt Sallie.

I shake my head. "I can't do that, Mr. Ashton. You know I can't. Let's just wait for the law."

CHAPTER 41

It seems like ages until we hear tires crunch on the drive above.

Ashton straightens and gives me a sad smile. "Thank heavens they came in through the exit. At least the diners won't be disturbed."

I can't believe it. After everything that's happened, Ashton is still worried about keeping up appearances.

There are footsteps on the stone stairs and then a knock on the front door.

I check the weapon to be sure the safety is off in case Ashton tries something, and then call out, "It's open."

Zandt enters first, followed by two uniforms I've never seen. I don't dare hope that Liam is with them. He isn't.

After Ashton is cuffed and led away, Zandt says, "We haven't located Liam yet, but I can assure you that we will. We have Ashton's contact in custody, and he's been spilling his guts."

Getting through the rest of the night is one of the worst stretches of time I've ever done.

It's Saturday. I'm out on my deck, looking down at the festivities unfolding below. After dinner comes dancing on the dock to CDs carefully chosen by Ashton—a mix of mostly oldies interspersed with a few new tunes played when dancing begins—until precisely eleven p.m. Everybody knows the young people will disappear as soon as humanly possible.

Poor Frederick Ashton. His life—and the life of the compound as its inhabitants know it—is over. Tomorrow, the news of his arrest will become the hot topic of Hotanawa's goodbye ritual.

I'm surprised when the wall phone rings from the hall. I head back inside and pick up, hoping for news from Liam.

"Hello?"

"Allie? It's Clarissa."

Why on earth is Clarissa Demme, née Napier, calling? Shouldn't she be down on the dock, drinking martinis and cursing the day I came to Hotanawa?

"Listen," she gushes, before I have time to respond. "I know everything. I got the whole story from Bo. I can't believe Ashton deceived us all as long as he did. I just wanted to say ... we just wanted to say ..."

Her voice trails off, and I catch genuine regret in it.

"Thank you," she says, finishing her sentence.

If I wasn't stunned before, now I'm really shocked.

"You're calling to say thank you? For what?"

She sighs. "For waking us up, Allie. For waking us up out of a trance."

I hardly know what to say as she invites me down for a farewell drink. This time, I accept.

I join the group on the boathouse dock until the final rounds of drinks are poured, and cigarettes are shared.

I can tell some of the others are angry, but they're also impressed. Impressed that I had the guts to do what none of them could do—dig beneath the surface, and see the façade of paradise for what it really was: a fraud.

I did it. I solved the mystery of Aunt Sallie's death, and helped shut down a pernicious meth operation in the process. I misjudged

Clarissa ... and Liam ... and Arlene ... and even Fin. We all make our mistakes, but it takes a particular kind of man to commit murder—a man like Frederick Ashton.

No one would have ever suspected him. But money, jealousy, and years of forbidden love make a man do crazy things.

After the other families and I say our goodbyes, the compound falls quiet except for the night breezes and the gentle lap of the lake against the shore.

It's well past midnight when I collapse onto the top of the king-size bed in the master bedroom, rolling from one side and then to the other several times before I find comfortable purchase and fall into an exhausted sleep.

Movement in the room barely disturbs me, nor does the sound of the shower beating against tile.

But when I feel Liam curl around me, I smile. Things are going to turn out just fine.

www.LouiseGaylord.com